The Tales of Magnus and Prime

A Fantasy Novel Series

Book Three:

Meeting of the Minds
Part 3

By Jack Robinson

magnusandprime.com

This is Paperback Edition 2018

First Edition

Printed by CreateSpace 2018

ISBN 978-1-9996060-2-2

Acting Out Ideas: A Foreword

Some fans and like-minded writers have asked me how to put ideas into words. So many of us have a great idea banging around our heads, but few ever take the time to express it. It's this kind of repression that can be potentially fatal for some of us. A good idea never acted upon leads to all kinds of depression and emptiness. I know this from my own experiences and it's god awful.

So, ideas? What should you do with them? Well, the best thing you can do is simple: catalogue them. It's strange to think one of the biggest solutions to an unhappy life is a piece of paper and a pen, but Occam's Razor is a very true thing. Pushing all your thoughts and ideas through your body and challenging them unto paper is only step one, however. In order to build anew you must first breakdown what already exists.

Step two: criticize and rework your ideas… a lot. The best works are those that you build up over time; no one concept is perfect from the start. This particular series of novels have each had seven drafts, including two complete rewrites.

Once you've ironed the flaws from your ideas, find the platform that best conveys them. Some turn their art to films, others comic books, and other still look to video games as a means to sell an idea. Personally, I love writing books.

There you have it: how to manage a head full of ideas. Coincidentally this little snippet of advice is how I turned my own cluttered head into a trilogy of stories. A trilogy I hope you have enjoyed and are looking forward to continuing in Volume 4 and beyond. After all, what good is an idea – what good is an act – without an audience?

Table of Contents

Meeting of the Minds
Vol. 3

By Jack Robinson

Prologue

Hericore sat under the Karin sun and weighed all of his bad choices against his eroding morality. With the Guard in pieces, he fought for a time over disbanding the group before more lives were ruined under their 'valiant' charge south.

His twisting train of thought was interrupted by the cawing of a raven cutting through the humid air. The bird was jet black and stuck out far too much in the bright desert land – casting covertness to the gentle winds. After circling the tents of the Guard, the raven perched on the drake's wing before cawing a few more times. With a note tied to its tiny neck, it refused to leave until it was relieved from its delivery. This message was destined for Hericore's eyes only.

However, with claws the size of sabres, Hericore's attempts to retrieve the note were fruitless and looked quite pathetic. As much as he'd love to ask for Philip's aid, the kid was yet to gain the drake's unconditional trust. Youth was a curse in its own right and one that can't be lifted easily, much like his own affliction. Wisdom was the only cure for youth and wisdom only came with age. Thus, Hericore sought a man of such age to retrieve his message.

He first though of Kenneth. The fisherman was still nursing a burn on his arm and trained with his sword continuously. It seemed he was motivated by something big – he was subject to a change of heart that was slowly turning a humble victim of fate into a weapon of it.

Hericore moved from Kenneth and left him to his training in the wispy hills that lingered on the town's outer edges.

Moving further from Declandale, Hericore spied the burnt out shack of the once cunning Greycoat, Patrick. Rick had survived his wounds, and did nothing but camp outside the ruins of his home in despair. The detective's life must've been similar to the families the Guard had ruined in Valordolt. For every step they took to King Barsalt's door a new widow was made and a few orphans joined her.

With shame infesting his cursed gut, Hericore bucked up and approached Rick. This simple task of getting a message off his wing turned into an hour of debate and history shared between the two. Hericore loved to yap away and those around him tended to share this love, but only while in his presence. Few men could resist a chat with the withered drake, whether it was to learn his past or his weaknesses, he still enjoyed every second of it.

Something was… off with Rick, something rotting within and something far deeper than his discoloured stomach wound. Souls were like books, easy to judge and a task to read, but all were readable in time. Something about Rick's book was troubling, with smudged pages and torn out passages. Hericore smiled along with him for now but kept an eye peeled. After Langdon, he wasn't going to be ambushed a second time.

By the time he'd left Rick to his ruins, Hericore almost forgot about the message he'd received from the crow. With the help of the Greycoat, he'd obtain the critical message from a friend pushed beyond his breaking point. Encoded in a language older than Magnus itself, it read:

Dearest Hericore,

I apologise for the crude method of delivery, sir. My days in the north have surely turned south.

The mission has fallen apart, and I'm afraid Ash has passed..

To add to the chaos, James is in captivity thanks to the Order and its pig-headed Battlemaster.

Luckily, the Stone is safe, and I'm seeking aid in my old classmate by the name of Edgar.

I may not be able to update you for some time, sir. I wish you the best in all you endeavours.

May the Guard bring purity to your curse and peace to this failing world.

-Zarpadon.

It was warming to hear of Zarpadon's safety, even if it was fleeting. But the feeling was numbed with news of Ash's demise. At the very start of their little brigade for the stones, Ash was one of the first people to back the idea, and even volunteered to lead the team north despite the risks involved. Did this make his death a fault of his own, or was Hericore just passing off his own streak of guilt?

Regardless, Hericore couldn't shake the feeling he was losing an impossible battle against fate, and his struggling only made the world a bloodier place. Maybe Magnus would be better off free from his own sense of justice and peace. After making another solid argument against himself, Hericore just stood under the sun and hung his head in shame. "This cannot continue," he sighed.

Chapter 1: The Mayor

Edgar Svanold, Mayor of Bridgeport, was perched his office chair, stroking his thick head of black hair. It pulled forward into a large quiff as he lathered on more grease, attempting to keep its erect form stable.

Since Wellington decided to set up shop in town, he'd not had a chance to keep well-coiffed; the Order rarely lent time to fashion.

Throwing on a dark, woollen coat over his faded orange shirt felt sinful. Locking his brightness behind a veil was a trend he'd kept throughout his life. Why, only now, did it feel so wrong?

His militant boots, tall and tightly laced, creaked all over when marching around the room, circling his desk and making several trips past a thin dress mirror. Cheap leather made for an audible nightmare, but fed cobblers who would've met a far worse nightmare than noisy footsteps had they lost their business.

The thrifty mayor's entire assembly of clothes was beggarly, according to his detractors. From trousers with mismatching patches on the knee to a garnet tie that never fit just right, many longed to see him laughed out of leadership. Maybe this was testament to his nature: never fitting, never matching.

Giving himself a once over in another mirror upon the desk, the plucky mayor winked at the sightly image. He loved his thin face and curved nose bestowed generously, ever thankful for life's little gifts. The perky smile was a nice touch too, a technique he'd dedicated years to perfect; women and men alike could appreciate a cheery face.

"Handsome as ever. Well, maybe not the ears," he admitted. "I could make an elf jealous."

Mayoral life contained limited respite, and with ribbons to cut and honours to dish out, Edgar's respite would have to wait. With tea in hand, he stared outside his window, and uptown Bridgeport stared back.

A personal clubhouse that spanned a mile, the place was a haven for artisans of all walks. Hundreds of playwrights were birthed and subsequently died each year in the bosom of Bridgeport's grace. The stage wasn't meant for everyone – but failure or no, Edgar was granted free entry to each and every performance.

Freebies were one of the few upsides of ruling, though the phrase 'ruling' was rather watered down in his case. The Order granted him power, but never too much, and they were determined to leash him tightly. No seat on The High Council belonged to young, 'foolish' Edgar, but that was fine; he'd always preferred the rosy streets here to the thorny alleys of Valordolt.

From the window, beds of delicate petunias, smoothed stone roads and beautiful views of the setting sun were visible over the horizon of thatched roofs; far better than the cobbled, piss-soaked setting Wellington called home. His city stood divided by the River Zest. North of the body of water was rich uptown, while in the south, the less fortunate folk of downtown Bridgeport lived.

Though Edgar hated the idea of a class-based living, it was a method that had worked for his father, grandfather, and so on, until the genesis of Bridgeport back in the third era. It would be nice to one day move on and usher in a new way of life, to demolish the traditional structure put in place by the Order and see the citizens of his city play on an equal field. But abolishing capital imbalance was one of several steps too far from his grasp, at the present. The staircase of politics every mortal was forced to climb was steep, and without an ensemble of friends to carry him, it was that much steeper.

Edgar was a rather lonely man, even given his tendency toward the extroverted. Gaining people's attention wasn't hard – it was getting them to stay without putting them in danger's way that he found so difficult. After a lapse of time, all those around him seemed to exit his life, one way or another.

But when the sun set over the various theatres and manors, the impossible was achieved, and for the first time in his life, an old friend flocked back into Edgar's company.

A flash of bright pink blanketed his peripheral vision, filling the glass pane on the office door. The silhouette of his guards fell with two loud thuds, and were replaced with a tall, pointed figure. Few crystivines would act so bravely as to stride through the front door, and only one was a wanted man.

"Zarpadon, I know it's you," Edgar called out to the figure, then whispered, "Not the most conspicuous arrival." Despite such aggressive actions against the guards, the angel had enough courtesy to knock before entering. "Come on in," the mayor said, jumping back to his chair.

Chipped and emanating less light than usual, his old friend looked disgruntled and could barely stand straight. He stumbled into the room and took a seat in the visitor's chair opposite. Much like Edgar's boots, the chair creaked under the crystivine's weight.

"Evening, Edgar," Zarpadon mustered weakly. The mayor kept his gaze busy, checking paperwork and nearby décor. Looking in the eyes of those around you was something Edgar hadn't quite mastered. Perhaps this awkward act was why so few stayed in his company.

"Greetings, old friend. You're looking well." Like a good smile, white lies also went a long way. "It's been what... Two years since we last met? I assume the crystals are treating you well? No creaking and the like."

"Two years? Far longer than that. You were still in school last time we crossed paths. And my crystals are doing well – aside from the hundreds of paladins hunting for them. But anyway, thanks for asking."

"Well then. Time does fly," Edgar pondered, confused as to where the time went, "but I don't need to tell *you* that."

Zarpadon's fatigue turned to suspicion at this hint.

"Rumours and nothing more," replied the crystivine, attempting to hide a long dead secret.

"Most people know of the curious incident at Palmer. No rumours there," Edgar said with smugness. "Would you be interested in some tea?"

"Tea? I don't even have a mouth, or throat, or–"

"Ah, of course; my mistake. I still find myself perplexed by your fascinating anatomy."

"You and I both."

Edgar still heated up the kettle upon its hotplate and prepared a cup for his lone self. How could the representative of Bridgeport not indulge in a little of the local export? The black pot turned orange under the pyrus plate's heat, and its water slowly bubbled away. He took this opportunity to question Zarpadon on his recent mishaps.

"So, what has gotten you in such turmoil with the Order?" he asked, while adding many spoonfuls of sugar to his cup.

With sugar came a sweetness he couldn't live without. At eight roths a bag, the expense was quickly outweighing the pleasure it purchased.

Zarpadon shifted in his chair. "Well, it starts right where the rumours end. My boss, the former Arch-Paladin, needed my help to save the world."

"And you couldn't resist?" Edgar said, knowing Zarpadon all too well. This guess was confirmed with a solemn nod.

"You bet. And I know you'd do the same." Demonstrating an equal knowledge of Edgar's own personality, the angel was spot on.

"I miss this. Me reading you like a worn book, all while you do the same."

When he was a freshman at Bridgeport's School of Business, more nights than not were spent with the then wandering angel. Before Hericore sunk a claw or two into him, Zarpadon was quite the talker – a joker, even. But that was then, and now? Now a stone-collared guardsmen was all that people saw in his friend.

"It's a bout of wondrous nostalgia, but I must get to the point. Lives hang in the balance," Zarpadon said in a sober manner.

A sad, but true fact; all of his fun seemed short-lived, and even the remembrance of fun carried the same curse.

"How can I help you, Zarp?"

"I need everything you've got on Wellington. Plans, locations, the whole works."

"A troublesome request. And how can I be sure you're not planning to assassinate him?" Edgar asked, never one for unwarranted violence. "You did release an assassin from her chains, after all."

"How did you-"

"I have *some* pull around here. Heard about the seven folks you sprung from shackles. A risky bunch you've befriended."

"Clearly you're not that connected." Edgar felt a wave of smugness being reflected back. Smugness, and something else. Something foreign to Zarpadon. "Haruka died in Ester Valley with the other prisoners. I simply want to save the survivors from the same fate. You're a good man, Edgar. I need a good man right now."

The plea was presented well, but the mayor's mind had been made up the second the door opened. He needed Zarpadon too, and this plea was just a pleasantry.

"I'll tell you everything, but I want something in return. A deal needs to be struck."

"What did you have in mind?" replied Zarpadon, in quick submission to his demand.

"I spill the news on Wellington's intentions, and in return you accompany me on a little excursion north."

"An excursion?"

"A religious trip to the Arcwoods; one I must make sooner rather than later. Something a long time coming."

As far as a religious trips went, this was stretching the meaning. But since Zarpadon didn't sound entirely truthful about the prisoners' deaths, Edgar felt it just to warp the truth behind his real intentions in the north.

"The magic woods hold few gods, Edgar. Honesty is a key quality of yours. Is this no longer true?"

"I never lie, Zarp. Especially to extra ordinary people, such as yourself."

"Then consider the deal well-struck," the angel replied, agreeing in another hasty manner. It seemed Edgar wasn't the only one sailing on desperate waters.

Moments passed, and the tea boiled, reaching its prime. He poured it, smelled the sweetness of the brew, and didn't wait to slurp it back.

"Doesn't that burn?"

"I've gotten accustomed to the heat."

As Edgar finished another mouthful, Zarpadon gazed over to the portraits on the wall – Svanold figures from eras past.

"Your father would be proud of this choice. He hated the Order more than most."

Edgar's father had been a busy man whose work and dedication drove him into the ground at an early age. He and pa weren't close, but did share this working drive – the lethality of efficiency.

"Maybe. But then, he also hated criminals too," the mayor added.

"I only look criminal because the Order has dressed me as one."

"They'll see you and your friends dead. I can't allow another death to occur in my city. I've kept Bridgeport murder-free for years now. I'm not breaking a record so rarely given," Edgar warned.

Drinking down more tea, he told an account of events from Wellington's arrival onward. "Your little stunt in Ester Valley cost the Order greatly. Wellington and Dirk have been in a frenzy since. Bridgeport has never seen religious traffic like this," he said, both grateful and worried about this extra activity. "The Battlemaster rode into town three days past, holding an orc on a leash, dragging him around town like a beast. I didn't realise it then, but your pal, James, was this orc."

"The savage. Ryon's the real beast here."

"Then when Wellington set up shop in the jail, I thought it would be ideal to find out why. Then your name came up. What took you so long to get here? We're nought but ten miles from Ester."

"Getting here wasn't the problem – hiding was. We spent half the day stuffed in an attic to avoid the Order's men. Slept right above Wellington, too," Zarpadon said, massaging his sore arms. Ester's survivors had clearly been though a lot getting in here incognito.

"Wellington's operating the manhunt from the jail. I can get you in and out, but only if honour is kept, along with your word."

In shock, Zarpadon leaned back, confounded.

"You'd betray the Order, just like that?"

"Yep, drop of the hat. Again, if you can help me out with my little project, I'll move mountains for you," Edgar said. "That, and Wellington is indeed a beast. If breaking James from his leash helps place it on Wellington, then I'm game."

The mad dog of the Order was reaching for sadistic goals beyond the scope of morality; few men killed their peers and got away with it. Edgar wasn't going to permit this reach. No one needed to suffer in his world.

"Good to know I'm not the only one to see Ryon for what he really is; proves my sanity in these troubled times," Zarpadon said with relief.

"Don't be too sure about your faculties. I've never claimed to be sane, myself."

When alone, Edgar found that his mind thought too much; humans made excellent grounding rods, only he was long overdue for a grounding. Such time had passed that he feared the fall from grounding at such a height.

"Maybe 'sane' is the wrong word for you, but intelligent was always spot on," Zarpadon complimented, sneaking in a sly chuckle.

"Oh, stop," Edgar replied coyly, "I'm no intellectual. Leadership often conflicts with scholarship."

"I recall you besting everyone in the academy, a feat even I couldn't claim. If leadership has dulled your mind, then you'll still be a genius." It was true – Edgar had the brainpower of a dozen men. It wasn't genetics that won him this prize, however, but pure dedication.

"Well, if you say so," the mayor weakly complied, staying humble.

"I know so. And I could use those brains in planning James' escape."

Zarpadon was charismatic, using compliments to lure cooperation from his lips. It wasn't compliments that won him over, but kindness. The angel was weak, and he wouldn't allow weakness to spell failure for his old friend.

"Fine, I'll help. First we need to discuss my half of the deal, and we only have a half-hour to do it." It was validated by a check of his father's old fob watch, an heirloom in name alone, as the sentiment was lost.

"Got somewhere to be?"

"I'm opening a pet store. Best not keep the public waiting." This garnered Edgar a funny look, but someone had to bestow their blessing on the shop; he very much doubted Wellington would. "Who's on the job this time? Lillian? Ash?"

"Neither. My team's different than usual, but effective all the same. We'll be able to extract James tonight. That's all I can give: all I have," Zarpadon summarised. "Now about this escort request?"

Edgar paused and prepared to drop a figurative bombshell, "This may sound grim, but I need help... 'ending' a god."

"What?!" yelled Zarpadon, almost breaking his monotone voice.

His reaction was most predictable. What Edgar asked was a grand task, but one well prepared for. A lifetime of work, he took the utmost decorum when discussing his heretical dream.

"You heard me. I need help to kill a god. A real Primal, that is. It'll be a lot easier than it sounds, trust me."

His friend stayed silent for a time, another expected response.

"Are you sure the pressure of being mayor hasn't fried your mind? Killing a god is near impossible. The only time it happened before was at the hands of another god. A mortal *would not* stand a chance."

Edgar smiled. "I never said we'd do the deed ourselves."

He opened the desk drawer and pulled out a wad of papers thicker than one of Bethany's Bibles. Placing it on top of the desk with a thump, the mayor proudly grinned. It was a lifetime of work in one place, his entire motive, reason, and planning expressed in written form.

Quickened by excitement, he started picking out specific pieces of paper, and handed them to Zarpadon. "Here, this summarises my mission."

The crystivine spent the next few minutes scanning through the notes and plans while they waited for another drink to boil.

Forgetting angelic biology again, he offered a biscuit to Zarpadon, only to be reminded of his lack of guts. "You really are missing out on the simple joys of life," Edgar said, crunching on a powder-coated cookie.

"I know you. This isn't you. These notes are far more than that," Zarpadon said. "Intelligent is a term ill-fitting of you, especially if you really want to pull this off."

"The joke about my sanity wasn't too exaggerated."

More papers were handed out, and more doubt filled the room. Edgar's planning was flawless. Failure relied only on the dwindling faith of his friend.

"Maps of solar cycles, the composition of light rays – this would imply you're targeting... Solaris?" Zarpadon gawked. "He's been in exile for decades. Finding him will take years, and you want him dead, too?"

Zarpadon saw only what Edgar wanted him to see, a mirage for his own protection. The real target of Edgar's quest was greater than the vilified exile Solaris. Gods were fickle things, unable to help the world. Man on the other hand... mankind was far from fickle.

"We've done our research, me and father. I want his power for my own. Gideon ripped it from Solaris upon his exile, as he did to Aldon. Now the former is a champions reward waiting to be claimed."

Zarpadon looked at him impassively. "Stealing a god's power? A goal of avarice."

"Stealing? No. It's simply a return to sender. I was born under the sun; I was born to wield the sun. It's claiming what is rightfully mine," Edgar clarified, adding entitlement to his rising megalomania.

After gaining the sun's strength, Solaris would live on again, in a twisted way; part god and part human. A twisted merging of Magnus and Prime.

"I suppose taking his removed power is easier than taking it from him directly," Zarpadon sighed, remaining sceptical.

"Exactly. He was banished to Magnus and lost most of his followers. His temple must be deserted by now. That's my first stop." He pulled a small book from the desk. "This is a translation script for all of Solaris' remaining scripture. Only his followers have one and can translate it. I spent a good deal of my adolescence acquiring one."

"So with this you could translate the work at his temple, yes?" Zarpadon confirmed.

"Nailed it! Prophecies, personal information and weaknesses all recorded in Sunscript, and locked behind a huge, bronze door. It's just waiting for me to uncover. All I need is you and your men to guide me there."

Gandering at the fob watch again, the mayor frowned. Time was short, and Zarpadon's doubt seemed too long to dispel.

"This is madness," the angel repeated. "This is a pointless power play. I... I can't just give the god's power to you. You're a good kid."

"Sounds like your lifetime of servitude speaking. You've seen their cruelty, first hand. Isn't it worth trying to stop it? I'm the man destined to end a corrupted rule. Aldon and Solaris are exiled, Aldrich is dead, and Hugo has fled. The gods aren't immortal, and they can be lassoed. Rules can apply to them."

"Hugo fled?" Zarpadon asked sharply.

Edgar hurried on. "Look, all I'm asking is for you to drop me off at the temple. You're already heading north, and I am freeing your friend."

Paces later, Zarpadon had finished debating.

"Fine. You've got yourself an escort." The crystivine caving in seemed under necessity, not want.

"Brilliant!" Edgar yelled, jumping out of his chair, followed by a dance around the office. "I can't tell you how long I've planned for this day. I'm getting all giddy now, that's new." He continued, throwing a key at Zarpadon. "That's for town hall's basement, your team can set up there. It's relatively abandoned, so... get going! I've got work to do."

Brimming with festivity, the young mayor danced through the doorway, out past his unconscious guards. Both girls looked safe, unharmed, and that was all that mattered. "Oh, and just leave these two. I'll make up some excuse about a prank gone rogue or something. Who cares, we're actually doing this! Catch you in an hour or two."

A heart full of hope gave Edgar the energy to sprint to the opening. Hope that one day, the dreams he'd grown up with would finally come to fruition, and the crown-less king would again sit on his throne.

Chapter 2: Old Friends, Old Problems

Zarpadon waited in the dank cellar for what seemed like an eternity. Rainwater dripped through the entry hatch, setting a calming backdrop within the aged room. Wine once filled the racks along the walls, but not for a long time. The smells of cherry and grapes remained, but the rest of the air was putrid; the painfully passive scent of moisture and dust.

Along with the wine racks were stacks upon stacks of old charts from Bridgeport's past. The records told of old land disputes with the Casterland, dating back to the eastern land's very inception.

Caster wasn't always so poetic with its culture, before migrating north. Old Caster was a religious hive of dark magic in the name of a faceless shade; a nasty past Zarpadon was glad to avoid.

The Casterlands weren't the only thing to waver in time. Edgar had changed, and the weird, wonderful boy he'd known was now a cracked visage of a man full of ambition, but at the cost of reason.

With a plan that managed to outrank Hericore's on the scale of impossibility awaiting Zarpadon's attention, every minute spent mulling over the task was extended, and ate at his nerves. He was saving James from a cruel execution, and still causing the distraction originally sought, but whatever Edgar was planning to do with a god's power was an enigma.

The clocks were almost striking midnight, and still they waited for the mayor's return. Krell and the twins had been briefed on the plot, and Edgar's sudden tardiness worried them all.

"The man of tweed and sunshine better not stab me. I'll stab the stabber back in his stabber's back," Krell muttered, over and over.

"Even the crazy one's getting restless," Kat said in boredom's name.

Since her encounter with the Time Stone, her actions seemed too dull, her words full of regret and movements laced with the embers of what was. Zarpadon's own journey back had been taxing on the soul, but not to Kat's magnitude. She was lifeless in most senses of the word. "I smell betrayal," she followed, sipping on her flask. Liquid Courage, much like the real stuff, ran in short supply after their time on the run.

"No need to fret. Edgar's probably putting things into motion. Like I said, he owes me a favour, or two by now," Zarpadon answered, examining the piles of old books left to stagnate in the dampness; a tragic waste of good paper.

Krell sat cross-legged, his head in the clouds, and Zarpadon wondered whether the madman's problems were due to a lack of emotion and awareness, or an overload. Either way, he wished to experience it – just for one day – and then maybe he could understand him.

Despite Krell's trauma, he was more talkative than Catherine, as of late. Since Kat's pondering state, her sister grew further and further away from the rest of reality. It was a feeling Zarpadon also would like to experience; maybe even adopt.

Back at Palmer, Sicilla had cracked him in two. His oldest friend on Magnus was no longer a part of Magnus. This ate at him for a thousand years, reaching depths once thought to be impossible to fathom. Eventually, he became more than crystivine, but not quite mortal. A hybrid of angel and man; a nephilim of loss.

That was until Hericore snapped him out the deep, removing the 'loss' part of his title, but only the loss. It was the promise of more, the promise of saving the world that broke his loss. But still, it almost cost him far more grief than he had any right to feel.

Shortly, the basement's hatch flung open, and Edgar ran down the stairs carrying several boxes in his arms, further warranting the big grin on his face.

"Where have you been? You said two hours," Zarpadon said scornfully.

Edgar's mouth lowered, and he dropped the boxes down on one of the room's many existing paper stacks.

"Sorry. I kind of got caught up at the opening ceremony. The pups there were just too cute to pass up."

"Dogs? While James, our friend, is sitting in a prison cell, you're busy petting dogs?!" Kat snapped. The mayor's warmth wasn't for everyone, especially the scornful and violent.

"Hey, calm down. I didn't spend the whole day petting dogs. They had birds too," Edgar replied. "And for your information, James is in a jail cell, not a prison cell. Clarification is key."

This wasn't the right answer, as Kat was turning redder by the second. "Seriously, you need to keep a cool head. Otherwise, this breakout's gonna go south real quick. I can't do anything to help you if Wellington catches us," the mayor added.

"So you have a plan then?" Zarpadon asked, attempting to place a wedge between them before Kat showed her claws.

"Check out box number one," Edgar said, grabbing the top box, hurling it into his grasp.

Inside were some maps of the city, including the Bridgeport jail cells, and a network of pipes that slithered under its surface. The prints looked old, signed by an architect with no recognisable title – simply 'Nova'.

"So we're entering from the sewers? Classic, but effective."

Edgar seemed offended by his analogy.

"The sewers, seriously? I have some class; I'm above such a filthy escape route. No, we're gonna leave through the flood canals. Clarification is key, remember?"

"Same difference."

"Me and dangerously blonde here are going to 'relieve' the jail's guards from duty, then you'll burn a hole from the flood canal to the cells with your magic."

Assuming the worst, Zarpadon was ready and willing to silence the jailers of Bridgeport with lethal force. Too long had he sat back while the rest of the Guard fought and died to the Order.

"I'll need a clean, precise shot, but I think I can collapse the whole darn jail," Zarpadon assured him, but Edgar wasn't impressed; a disapproving look was all he garnered.

"Ah, murder… A dash of southern hospitality, I see."

Zarpadon bristled. "Southern? I'm from the heavens, not some desert. I'm not giving the Order any more slack: no more chances."

"Yes, but Prime has a south too. Not my fault I grew up with some class. That's why we're doing it my way: in and out with no killing."

"That's no how we play," Kat interrupted, exchanging a determined look with her twin. Kat was ferrying a false facade, using her 'courage' to force a fearful face; not that Edgar was fazed.

"Then you best learn the new rules, blondie. Because my word is law here. No killing."

"My blade could disagree with you, beanpole."

"And when I disappear off the face of Magnus, the Order will find you that much quicker." Edgar was stern and repeated his goal with a sharp stare. A fire appeared in the boys hazel eyes, a subtle fury that caused his right eye to twitch. "No–killing."

Kat didn't give an inch, and to save Edgar and the mission, Zarpadon stepped back in. "I'm from the north of Prime."

"That's enough, Zarp. Let it go," nodded Edgar, finally backing away from Kat's intense stare. He didn't fully believe she'd draw her blade, but why risk it all on a something as temperamental as faith?

"Why deal with the guards at all? Let's just enter through the sew-" Zarpadon paused to see Edgar's eye twitch ever so slightly, "-flood canals."

"I have maps of the city, but have no idea which cell James is kept in. You can use me as a beacon. Tracer spells are still in your repertoire, I hope."

Part of using the arcane arts meant Zarpadon could place a 'tracer' on another source of arcus: the very make-up of arcane magic, especially prevalent in mortal blood. With enough attunement on the caster's part, such a spell could track a man and his blood across the planet.

"It's been a while since my last tracer. I'll try my best, though," the crystivine assured him. Edgar gave a thumbs up, then turned to the twins.

"Ever broke into a high-security building before, girls?"

"I'm a Ganger," Kat sneered. "Getting in won't be a problem. Disguises are my forte."

"Aggressive and deceptive. I like you."

"Watch what you say. I love to live up to the aggressive part," Kat lashed out at the flattery.

Catherine finally spoke up and asked, "Were do I fit in with this?" Her voice was still croaky and weak. Tears came easily to the girl.

"Well darling, you and Krell will be manning the escape boat out at the docks. It's a foolproof plan," Edgar said, with a clap of the hands.

"Never call her 'darling'. *Ever*," Kat threatened.

Edgar gulped. "Noted."

For all the negativity, the twins seemed to tolerate Edgar – this increased with each sentence spoken. The mayor had a way with words that bordered on the supernatural. Maybe this was why they were so willing to kill a god?

"Why can't I join Kat? We're both Gangers. We work well as a duo," Catherine suggested. Zarpadon backed her point. Kat was still full of rage, and needed her sister more than ever.

"Okay then, the ladies are with me. Now let's discuss the trip to Solaris' temple."

James was a good friend, just as much an asset, and the angel struggled with Edgar's lazy summary of the breakout. The orc wasn't going to be lost at poor preparation's hands.

"Can we finish talking about James' escape first?" he asked Edgar, only to be met with a blank stare.

"We did, Zarp. We come in from below, and leave from below; end of story."

"That can't be it," he argued. "'Clarification is key', after all."

Edgar let out a revealing sigh.

"There's no time. See, another niggling detail I found out while prowling the puppy-filled opening event was the Order's plans for James and company. Wellington's pulling back to Valordolt tomorrow, and they're coming with him."

"Wait, they're leaving tomorrow? How have they given up already?!" Kat yelled.

"Can you keep it down? You're all *fugitives*!" Edgar yelled back. "There's been a mutiny of sorts in Refracted Light. Wellington's needed to keep the peace; that's all I've heard on the matter, and frankly that's all we need to know."

It hadn't occurred to Zarpadon that the enemy had a home to fight for, too. He himself also fought for the same land, Valordolt, the shining apple of Bethany's eye. Two factions were fighting under the same banner, yet at each other's throats. A productive waste of what little time remained.

"That's why we need to get James out tonight. I suggest that we skip the finer details and talk about the temple.. *now*," Edgar wrapped up, as he grabbed the second box from the pile and handed it over.

Inside was a map of the Arcwoods, and a small, golden disc with a sun carved onto it. No bigger than his palm, it gave a dim light to the world around it. Grasping the disc yielded a strange, warmth, one of divine power and will. "That's a key straight into the temple. Like I said, I've been planning this for a while now," Edgar said, bloating further on pride.

"Good enough. I'm ready," said Kat, hinting at restlessness.

"Me too," Catherine said, with much less attitude.

Zarpadon disliked the haste involved, but had little choice.

"Clarity will have to wait, I suppose."

"Music to my ears," Edgar clapped. "Any final words before we depart?" The room went silent, followed by Catherine's meek, raised hand.

"Yes, I have a question. You're the mayor. Surely you could muster up your own force. The amount of swords around town is overwhelming."

"Oh, I like you. More so than blondie. Curiosity can kill you if you're not careful."

"It can try," she said back, bouncing off the mayor's wit like rubber.

"I couldn't use my own men. I could, if the town's guard weren't supplied by the Order. They worship Bethany, and I'm trying to kill her husband. It's not an act they'd be fond of. But good question. Benign, but still good."

Kat shot looks of dislike at Edgar's advances. The mayor was doing what he did best: sweeping people away with a slue of charisma. Like him or not, Edgar was here to stay for a while.

Zarpadon wanted the boy he knew to return, but this was a pipe dream, something he'd have to live without. All boys became men eventually, and Edgar was just participating in nature's grand play – a play that was reaching an abrupt end.

Chapter 3: Bridgeport Breakout

Edgar led the girls to James' captivity, requiring them to cross over from uptown to downtown Bridgeport, a breaching of the classes. The only way to achieve this was by crossing the Breach, a lengthy, iron bridge that clung to each bank of the River Zest, which cut the city in two.

The biggest sight to see in Bridgeport, the Breach was a marvel to behold; such raw tensile strength hanging above the fluid river below was a clash of two beauties. This clash continued in the bridge's support, with both sturdy pillars below and swaying suspenders above. Seeing the steel meander from its place resonated with Edgar's own wanderlust, and his sheltered scientific mind tingled at the engineering feat the Breach stood as. Man achieved more than most, a fact lost on the other races of Magnus.

Lining the Breach were arcus-lit advertisements, displaying all manner of products brewed and crafted locally, from purging cure-alls to alcohol that turned the drinker into a dragon – if only in fiery might. Consumerism was another glorious sight to behold, another gift given to the world by man, who'd been able to transform jealousy into a more productive trait: greed.

Kat didn't look as impressed. Her glamoured face frowned at the billboards and their dedication to want.

"What's the point in showing off half this crap?" she asked, shielding her eyes from the bright signs that flickered rapidly.

"People always find new things to waste their hard-earned roths on. I just make sure it's all spent on useful things, rather than more… illicit items."

"You count stuff that makes your dick hard as 'useful'?" She pointed out an ad for Woodworkers, 'a potion guaranteed to make your wood easier to whittle'.

"Well, not me personally, but some people need it," Edgar nervously countered.

"Sure. Best grab an Arc-Mech 'escort' while you're at it," she mocked, pointing out another lewd poster.

As Kat became friendlier with him, the more she pushed the limits of what could be considered 'nice'. Luckily for Edgar's bravado, Catherine broke her sister's light-hearted abuse with a valid question.

"Who are we right now?" she asked, looking over her new body, wrapped in Bridgeport colours.

"Since Zarp decided to knock my guards about, I saw no guilt in taking a hair or two off them. They're tough girls, they won't notice anything amiss," he answered. "Why do you ask? Looking for a re-roll?"

"Not at all. I'm loving the new look – plumper than usual, but the smooth skin is a real treat. The hair's a little fiery for my tastes," Catherine replied, tampering with her temporary visage.

Paladin patrols grew more frequent the closer they came to their prize; none second-guessed the girls' glamours, but they still put Edgar on a fine edge.

"Why didn't you change your genders too? Seems like it'd make you harder still to detect," he whispered. "I'd very much like to stay incognito."

"Glamours only change appearance. Transmorphogens are what we'd use to change into a guy. We call 'em Trans-Gens," Kat educated.

"Never heard of the stuff," the mayor muttered. Trans-Gen sounded like shady operation offered by an even shadier surgeon roaming the back alleys of Valordolt.

"Not surprised. It's hard to brew, expensive, and dangerous to boot," Catherine said. "Plus mixing the stuff with the effects of a glamour can cause seriously unhealthy reactions."

"Last thing I need is to have my guts burned through like parchment," Kat brutishly added.

"Sounds delightful," he grimaced. "Why would you ever subject yourself to such a thing?"

"The gods are cruel, plain and simple. Not every guy wished to be born a guy, and vice versa. Trans-Gens are there to help fix what those above cannot."

Edgar thought for a moment. "I never thought someone could be so alienated from birth."

"Neither did the gods, apparently."

He stopped for second, and gazed at the blue marble in the night sky. Prime never looked real from a distance, with a glazed appearance similar to a marble.

It wasn't until then that he believed Prime to be a false world. Troubles, real troubles, never reached the tiny orb. They despised the unclean nature of mortality, and had become bigots in the wake of purity.

***

Kat started acting more paranoid than usual. Constantly she turned her head, looking for any flaw in the plan. A lack of confidence could be useful, but risky.

"You doing okay, Kat?" Edgar asked, with kindly tones.

After the address, she snapped back, "Don't call me that. If someone hears–"

"No one's gonna hear us. It's one in the morning, all of downtown's residence are sleeping off a night of thick inebriation." But Kat didn't calm down – she clenched the hilt of her holstered blade even tighter and continued to search for possible threats.

"Fine. But for now, call me something else. A code name, like... Beth. Call me Beth."

When the word 'Beth' hit him, Edgar's body tightened, then calmed to a place of emptiness.

"I'm not calling you that. A lot of bad memories with that name."

"An ex-lover?" Kat guessed.

"Of a sort. More of a wife. And definitely not an *ex-wife*."

Beth may have left him, but her charms still gripped around Edgar like a caring shackle. Their separation was too long, even for a man as stead-fast as he. Holding hope close, the day would come when they'd met again; the tales always ended with the lovers victorious.

"Shit, never pegged you for the marrying type," Kat said with disbelief.

"You look too young," added Catherine.

"Age can be deceiving. Ever heard the legend of Short-Fuse?" Edgar said, sagely.

They both declined, with a synced, "Who?"

"To him, age was really just a number; a great big number."

"Whatever, I'm sure he's a great guy. I'm still keeping Beth. Deal with it," Kat said, caring little for living legends. Her spirit was dangerous, even in Edgar's company. She tickled the hands that pulled her from a deep chasm – not the best idea.

"Okay then, *Beth*. What about you, Catherine? Got any 'code-names' you'd like to use?" he said, poking fun at the whole idea.

"Jane's good. Jane and Beth?" she answered, looking for her sister's approval.

Kat shrugged her new, bulking shoulders.

"Sure. Whatever works."

Fake names chosen, they soon stood facing the jail's navy doors. Two of Wellington's crusaders stood to either side, and looked pleased to see him.

The mayor knew the two from years ago, before they joined the Order, when they'd served under his father. Like Zarpadon, they were lost friends from his past, and he'd used this to gain easy access to the building.

"Phineas, Stanley, good to see you. It's been what, three years since we last met?" Edgar said, with open arms, brimming with false happiness.

The two smiled, but did nothing more. The taller, more muscular man, Stanley, spoke to him. Stepping forward, Stanley brushed aside his hair, a raggedy, white mop of wires, and bowed graciously. It was proper, but unbalanced thanks to the soldier's crocked knee, earned proudly along with several deep facial scars. Fighting the Drakeguard was a sport to some.

"Mayor Svanold, it's a pleasure, as always. It's been a lot more than three years, Sir."

"Time's lost on me," the mayor replied.

"Indeed. May I ask what you're doing here this late at night?"

His mind drew a blank and erred. He'd failed to create an actual 'why'; the truth wouldn't suffice, and a bad lie could be the trio's undoing.

"I just swung by to see... the... prisoner. Yes, I'm here to see James," he blurted out. It was a hasty move that could cost him greatly, but all the mayor could muster.

Stanley looked at him suspiciously, and asked a follow-up question.

"And why do you want to see Master Wellington's prisoner?" Edgar took another moment to ponder more thoroughly; removing the hesitation on this second decision.

He knew Stanley and Phineas were always quiet men, unsociable ones. A closed pair, they cared little for the rest of Wellington's knights. After pulling the pieces together, the puzzling problem was no more.

"Beth, my guard, lost her brother to the murdering swine. I thought she deserved some closure. To confront the killer in a safe manner," he replied, and awaited Stanley's verdict.

Tensions rose as the seconds ticked by, and Kat refrained from any irrational movements during the wait. The worst thing she could do was make a sudden jerk for her sword.

"Who was he, her brother?" asked Stanley. "Might've known the poor sod."

Of all the paladins he'd met in service to Bethany, none came to mind, until a rather dull memory struck him.

"Lud?" he slowly said. "Lud Kavel."

Stanley returned to Phineas' side, and the two whispered between themselves, battling loyalty against friendship. After more tension had been raised, they opened the door to the building.

"Right this way," Stanley said, gesturing towards the open door. Edgar smiled, thanked the duo, and wished Phineas well, as Stanley escorted them inside.

The corridors in the jail were claustrophobic to say the least. How a bulking giant like James squeezed through them was unknown to him, as even Stanley had to move at an angle throughout.

Along the way, a couple of elite troops watched over the barred doors to the central rooms. They were monstrosities in black-iron, plugged into a fancy meld of science and smithing that imbued them with a purple hue; the sign of an electromancer.

They wore huge generators on their backs that conducted the power of lightning from tanks of electrone crystals, channelling it to their gauntlets. Adding to their already large build were lengths of ineffective, naked wires sure to be a hazard to all involved.

"What are they?" whispered Kat.

"Shock troopers," Edgar replied. "The Order thinks Zarpadon's planning a breakout. What's the one weakness of arcane magic? Lightning."

"That's barbaric. Zarp's made of the pink stuff; one good jolt could kill him."

"Wellington doesn't care. He offed Gaffer without mercy. Why would Zarpadon be any different?" Catherine said.

"I'm going to kill him, and his walking lighting rods," Kat claimed, her speech becoming louder.

"Shh, If you do, then we all die with him," the mayor reasoned quietly.

"We're here. Keep your hands in view at all times and we'll have no problems," exclaimed Stanley, as he fumbled his old fingers around a locked door that opened into the jail-house proper.

The cells were in a much wider room than the corridors, and leaned against the south wall of the building. There were four cages in total, two empty, one containing James, and the final one was filled by an elderly molluskan.

The room wasn't empty. Wellington himself was sitting on a small wooden chair that looked fatigued under his weight, creaking as he leaned back against the wall to the left.

Lastly, a young, red-headed boy was sitting at a table beside the Battlemaster that had many empty ale bottles atop it. The smell of hops filled the air, prominently from Wellington's corner. The Battlemaster was drinking again, and using his teenage squire as an inadequate bartender.

In the cell, James had a long grin on his face – an odd emotion for the orc, given the circumstances. As for the molluskan? The only expressions made were negative ones.

"Edgar! Good to see ya," Wellington cheered. The brute rose to the occasion, knocking the table of liquor forward a half foot. "Would you like a drink? We got Ivory cider, Karin wine, and even a stash of Drakescale. You interested?"

Edgar was surprised at the sheer amount of booze Wellington had for a week-long trip – and this was only what remained, after the brute had already drunk several fills.

"I'm fine, Ryon. Just finishing some business before bed," the mayor replied, keeping the liquor at arm's length.

"Shame. Damn shame."

Much to his displeasure, the Battlemaster staggered over and wrapped an arm over his shoulder, giving Edgar a hefty whiff of bad odour. "What about your beautiful guards? Bet you hand-picked those babes yourself," Ryon asked, eyeing up Catherine's chest.

She blushed and turned away, as would any sane soul courted by the barbarian. Edgar's own libido was a mite on the back of Wellington's colossal drive. The beast had no control, but seemed to enjoy such lust; more than Edgar could say about it.

"Look, Willy," Wellington said the squire, "another ginger. You should get on that ride before she's hitched!" The boy just stared at his slurring lord in a fearful way. The kid didn't want to be there; maybe more so than he. "Nice pair of 'pairs' you've picked like pears. B*onvo et ciao, mon beau cher*," Wellington rhymed, congratulating him. The giddy tone in Wellington's voice was more unbearable than his stench, and his joy seemed as unnatural as James' smile.

"You have no idea," Edgar replied. "They're actually why I owe you the visit. One of them lost a brother to that orcish murderer, and I was hoping she could meet the monster." With a chuckle of acceptance, Wellington released him, and moved over to the twins.

"So, which of you lovely ladies has James 'ere to thank for ya grief?"

Kat stepped forward, with a voice of pure ire she answered, "Me."

Chapter 4: Facing the Devil

Kat swallowed her proud vengeance and stepped up to Gaffer's killer, wondering if she was capable of enduring him; a risk she'd have to take.

"Hello, my lovely. Can't say I've seen your good looks around. To whom do I owe this pleasure?" Wellington continued to slur in his slumbering state.

She was never comfortable in her own skin, and the comfort she felt as Helena was repeated now as Beth. With such comfort, facing Gaffer's killer became somewhat bearable.

"You owe Beth. You owe her a great deal. I lost my brother to the orc. He's no more than a monster, dressed as a man," Kat said, diverting the remaining anger from Wellington and aiming it in James' direction. Not only was redirection good for playing a convincing role, but also would keep her from reaching for the irrational.

"Hear that, murderer?! You killed her kin and spirit in one blow. Unholy savage!" Wellington yelled at James. The giant didn't seem to care. He kept his grin, and giggled a little at the rise in voice. "Excuse his unsympathetic nature, milady," Wellington apologised. "I had Stan spike his dinner with some quint powder. Thought it'd loosen his tongue. It did – but in all the wrong ways. The bastard's been on a high ever since, and keeps singing queer tunes of heresy."

Quint powder was something Kat never wanted to hear of again. Past romps around the Wasternland had given her more insight on this drug than she'd ever wanted.

The illegal spawn of opium and magic, quint was known as the 'glass bird' – the feather-shaped crystals could raise any man to unimaginable heights. The serious isolation from reality could seem fun at first, but one bad hit, and your life was cancelled.

Quint's allure stole Flan from her – it only made sense that Wellington would use such a menacing substance.

"Ryon, can we just get this over with? I want to go home and wind down," Edgar asked.

"Aye, I bet you do. I'd love to end the night with two thick an' chesty lasses, myself."

Kat resistance of Wellington's 'charm' was a losing battle, kept alive by Edgar's grounding presence. Revenge had a strong pull, but the mayor's light was enough to hold it off – barely. "The orc makes my ears bleed from his broken tones, but he's still a cut above the Ganger down there. A sinner, plain and true."

In the far cell sat Opyus, stripped to the shell, removed from all clerical uniform. He was also drugged into a fleeting state of will, though lightly compared to James. The battered molluskan had fought against Wellington's claims and chemicals; a bold fish, even when beached.

"We all sin," claimed Opyus, "and my shameful deeds are nothing compared to the rise of sin that encapsulates your existence."

"I am a man of Bethany. You lost that privilege by profaning honour and trust alike. Only the title of traitor fits you."

"Good. The title of deacon never interested me. As a *traitor*, I still hold more honour than you, boy." In relaxation, the molluskan threw himself onto the cell's lice-covered bed, and waited for the Battlemaster's response.

"Watch that tongue, Kraken, or I'll rip it from that disguising those jowls of yours."

"Proving my argument is no counter-argument. Surely a tactical man such as yourself, would've known that," Opyus retorted.

"Shrouded on the shore..." James joyfully sung, interrupting the heated squabble. "Looking out, to the edge of tomorrow!"

"Bethany give me strength! I ought to kill you both right now!" roared Wellington.

"You'd have a hard time trying," Kat let slip.

"Why? You'd stop me, *girl*?"

"Ryon, please. She wants to see them suffer for her loss, just as you do. Grief is wavering her will, that's all. You of all people should know what that's like," Edgar said. The mayor then directed himself at her. "Dancing with danger can be a devil's delight. I hope *everyone* can calm down and use such insight."

A not so subtle jab at her returning aggression, Kat cooled herself, grit her teeth, and apologised. Wellington did the same, as did James. Opyus was the only one to scoff, still rebelling for his lost cause. Kat moved in front of the cell, and the squire was sent away to fetch a dose of ground electrone crystals: a gem that was part magic and part drug, much like Flan's old attraction to pyrus.

Doctors the world over believed the mind was a net of lightning, constantly erupting with bursts of thought and memory. Some claimed to have even jumped into their minds and seen such a shocking sight. Crazy though it was, Kat had some faith in the fallible logic – faith coming from how people reacted to electrone.

The only way she used to avoid a quint-induced come-down was to purge her head with the elemental gem: a jolt to the mind's net, causing great pain along with its practicality.

"This brother. Was he pure of heart?" asked Wellington. Gaffer was pure, in the same way alcohol was, and Kat would have it no other way.

"He was a drunkard and a fiend. But pure, all the same."

Wellington nodded. "I would've liked him then?"

"You'd probably kill the blighter," she jabbed.

"I did kill him, like the rest of 'em, all gone because some cracked drake wanted to play the hero," Wellington said, ashamed of his words. "Can't blame him. I'd do the same if the Order commanded it."

Since their first encounter and the seeds of hate were sown, this was her first agreement with the Battlemaster.

Hericore, the blithering lizard who'd set this all in motion, was to blame. He hired the Gangers, betrayed the Order, set up the ambush. Gaffer died for Hericore's cause, which held the same weight as Opyus' now; all smoke with no fire.

"Yep, we few fools," Kat replied.

Zarpadon must be skulking below, needing an indication of where to aim his destructive magic. The tracer was placed on all three of them, its power leaving a deep hum within her stomach, growing strong as the crystivine closed in.

It was violating in a way, part of another leeching onto her very being. It was a necessary violation, however, unlike the downpour of sleaze Wellington doused her and Catherine with.

"Beth, Jane, did I ever tell you girls about the tunnels that run beneath the city?" Edgar asked, in a discreet manner.

"Never. What about them?" asked Catherine inquisitively, acting the fool.

"Well, apparently the construction crew in charge of building them were so lazy, they only dug them a few feet below the flooring plans. Rumour has it, that on a quiet night you can hear a monstrous creature *stomping* around down there." Stomping being the operative word, Kat knew what needed to be done.

"How interesting, Sir," she replied.

"Load of codswallop, that is. Me mum always used to say that, too. An old wives' tale," Wellington said as he cracked open another bottle and took a sip of the pale ale.

The moron was oblivious to their goals, his vision obscured by a haze of spirits. It would've been a flawless operation; 'would've' being the operative word.

Kat moved even closer to the iron bars, awaiting the perfect opportunity to make some noise. When she approached, James snapped back into action and sparked up a sloppy conversation.

"Hello there, sugar cheeks. Have we met?" he asked.

"No, but you've met my brother, to whom you gave the sword."

"Saddens me to hear this. 'Twas just business, an all. I've lost some friends too." James said this in a slowed pace, breathing heavily from his high.

"Who could you have lost? Orcs seldom make friends," Kat asked sceptically, a question that he was more than willing to answer.

"Oooh, about a year ago, me and my friends had to rescue some of the Order's stiffs from a fort inhabited by vampires..." Slowly, he broke into an inaudible mumble. After a few mumbled lines he giggled some more and recited another hazy fragment of his past. "Quit calling me Pebbles, new kid. Ha! I'm more than that. I'm a boulder!"

At the mention of the secretive mission, Wellington also started to have an interest in the story.

"Go on, orc. Tell me what really happened at Palmer," he asked, joining Kat and filling the air with tainted musk.

"Not you. This is sugar cheeks' story," James spat out, promptly silencing on the topic.

"Fine, be an ass. It's your traitor head on the line. Not that confessing will save that rock hide," Wellington leered, then moved back to the table of booze, keeping an obvious ear in the chat.

"So, we lost people," James continued. "Our analyst, Sicilla, was torn apart during an explosion, and my pet crayfish, Gerard, he was lost to the passage of time." This was told with a flurry of elastic emotion, streaks of sadness and repressed aggression. "He was so cute, with his little whiskers flittering in the light. He'd already died once and I had him resurrected by Travis. The poor... little... fishy. Dead like the rest of us if Ryon gets his way."

All the absurd talk of zombie crayfish was amusing to Kat, but annoying to Wellington. Blood could be seen rushing to his shiny dome, the symbol of hot headed endeavours.

"Pure bollocks! Tell the truth, traitor. What are you, Hericore, and all the other rejects planning?" he shouted, spilling his drink over his heavy armour plating and stumbling over his own feet. "I knew that wimpy, dandy shit had something cooking. Was it a coup? A murder? What act of terrorism were you planning?"

The drunk's words were growing more desperate and hasty. He carried on, slowly ticking off the possible ploys the Drakeguard could've implemented. With each empty accusation, Kat's façade cracked.

The Battlemaster's voice was so mighty for a man of little might, too high for such a low-blowing murderer. Ryon Wellington equated to a slug, always trying to be a tall loin in armour, reaching up for the bright stars while creating a void of blackness beneath him; abuse of power at its finest. "Tell me what is hiding behind that grin, or I'll peel it back and see for myself!" he continued, threatening James repeatedly.

"Nothing but brains behind this grin. Can't say the same for you," James replied, widening the grin, if only to taunt him.

"Bethany have mercy. Cos I sure as hell won't."

Kat focused on the little things to retract from her sick thoughts. She closed her eyes, hearing Opyus' humming, Edgar's rambled attempts to reason with Wellington, and her sister's fingers tapping on a crossbow, ready to strike.

It was then, amidst the chaos, that she had a truly ingenious idea: she'd get the mad dog to signal Zarpadon for them. The irony in his defeat would only be silenced by her blade – a fitting end, dishonour to the dishonourable.

"Wellington, this man, this traitor, has killed dozens of your own, and now mocks your very position as leader. You need to teach him a lesson," she commanded, playing the devil's advocate and angel's justice simultaneously.

Sparks ignited a fire in Ryon's belly, and after those words of encouragement, the Battlemaster finished his pint and yanked open the door that confined James.

Stanley joined Edgar in trying to be a voice of reason – but it was failing.

"My Lord, do you think brawling with the prisoner is a good idea? Remember when you killed–"

"Stan, if you don't shut up, right now, I'll have you and your pal, Phineas, cleaning the Citadel's latrines till your fingers become one with the shit you scrub!" Wellington barked as he fumbled for his sword.

"But what about Beth's talk?" Edgar asked. "You owe her a life. Her brother's life."

"With no due respect, Ed, you're gonna have to wait for this 'closure'. I'm afraid ol' James is gonna give it through a broken set of teeth."

Thrusting the door off its rusted hinges, Wellington threw a few poorly-angled punches at the ten-foot giant. James didn't defend himself, but didn't really need too; the drunken punches could barely break past his stony skin. Noise echoed throughout the building and down into the tunnels.

Edgar stopped his talk, clicked the pieces together, and darted over to Kat with glee in his face.

"Brilliance. Pure, untapped brilliance. You, you're my new favourite," he said, with a peck on the cheek, only to retract in a grimace. "Urgh, not quite sugary though." Embarrassed, yet pleased, Kat watched her efforts play out; act two of a three part spectacle.

Zarpadon heard what he needed to blast a hole clean under James, and got to work burrowing through the stone floor, spinning glowing, pink beams of arcane energy across the floor.

At this point, Stanley knew what was awry, and sought to rally reinforcements from outside the dingy room. Kat saw her sister's arms rise, taking aim at the old man, to which Edgar didn't approve.

"Catherine. No!" he yelled, but to no avail.

Her sister, ruthless in judgement, didn't give Stanley the chance to run, placing a bolt straight through his head. Stanley gurgled and dropped like a bag of rocks.

Wellington paid no mind, busy working James' stomach now, all while the giant laughed childishly, replaying a rendition of 'A Siren's Shanty'.

"Oh, three men set straight sail for the port of Ceequale–" The shock troopers' booming footsteps eventually closed in on the room and the racket; time was now of the essence.

"You didn't have to kill him!" Edgar shouted, scolding Catherine's actions.

"So perfect Kat can rip a girl apart, but I can't save my friends?!"

Kat never believed that she could be the favoured child until now. Even with all her failures, she still was treated better than Catherine. Maybe Gaffer wasn't the ass he appeared to be – if so, Wellington needed to pay twice over for his crime.

Jumping into the beat-down, Kat wrapped an arm around Wellington's neck, and gave the Order's dog the beatdown he deserved.

"A hundred good people die every day," she whispered. "Just this once, stop pretending to be one of them."

But as she pulled back her sword and poised for the kill, the floor shone pink, and crumbled at their feet, sending them both falling into the tunnels. Her vision went black, then red, as she embraced her lust once more and set out to coat her new face the classic shade of bloody crimson.

Chapter 5: Demon Slayer

Edgar stood frozen in the rampage Kat had orchestrated; a hastily constructed palace of poor choices and failure. Catherine was quick to follow her sibling into the canal's dim setting, diving for the hole before the dust had settled, leaving him alone in the room.

He glanced back at the destruction that transpired, and couldn't help but think that this was his jail, in his city. The people of Bridgeport had been failed, all because a poor choice of friends on his part.

With Stanley's blood pooling at his feet, a plague of remorse grabbed Edgar's mind, but the allure of his life's goal was too strong, and acted as a beacon in this grim storm.

"I'm coming home," Edgar said with a feeling of warming happiness, and joined the others in the tunnel.

Dropping down, he managed to situate himself with ease, repositioning his hairstyle accordingly. Catherine panicked over her missing sister, shouting out for her alongside Opyus, and Zarpadon had problems moving their ally, with James acting lethargic in his high state, refusing to stand of his own volition.

"Right," Edgar clapped, "we need a new plan." This announcement opened the conversation to everyone. "Any ideas? Anyone?"

His cringing look didn't exactly inspire anyone, and nary a person humoured his question, instead doubling their efforts to move James, and locate Kat.

A ghost audience had never discouraged him before, and he continued thinking out loud. "Ah, well, we need to find which way is north. That will lead us to the river."

Sticking a finger in his mouth, he then presented it to the winds of the tunnel, which held surprisingly little strength, tickling the tip of his index. "We need to head that-a-way..." he cheered, pointing down the brighter side of the tunnel.

"I can't," denied Catherine. "Kat ran the other way, after Wellington." A siblings love was unconditional, and stronger than anything Edgar could say in discouragement.

"I know it's hard to hear this, Catherine, but you need to get to safety. That's what Kat will want for you."

"I can't leave her; she's a danger to herself, now."

"I'm not asking you to – I'm ordering you," he said, placing his finger over her soft lips, halting any more complaints. "I'll look for Kat myself, while you lead the others topside. Time to take action, darling."

Catherine's lower lip quivered. "You promise to save her?"

"I'll up the ante and even save Wellington."

"But can I trust you?" Her panicked words started to rest, and her beautiful softness returned.

"I *promise*," he reassured her. "Cross my heart."

It was a bold claim that he hoped would hold true. Without allowing Catherine time to disobey again, the mayor paced away down the metal tubing, away from the light, and into a dark embrace.

***

The winds soon picked up the deeper Edgar travelled. They sung the most epic choir, whirling around the tunnels, masking all distant sounds, and filling his eardrums with the sweetest melody. This choir was quickly blocked out by a close patter of footsteps following him.

In pursuit was the elder molluskan who Zarpadon had called Opyus. A spry old man, Opyus chased him through the labyrinth, losing what little energy remained inside him.

"You should turn back. This might get hectic. An oldie like yourself can easily fall behind," Edgar kindly warned him.

"Can't do that. You need me, kid," claimed Opyus, as he caught an elusive breath. The old man's body was weak and slowly getting weaker; he would only hold back the gallant rescue.

"I made a promise," Edgar reminded him, "to get everyone to safety."

"You promised to save your friends and your enemies. I am neither."

"Not possible. I don't believe in neutrality; it muddies otherwise crystal clear waters."

"Then does it matter what I am to you? You'll protect me either way." Opyus said, turning the mayor's upstanding morals back on themselves.

"It always matters what you are. People are too eager to cast off their importance these days – becoming a martyr for no reason other than it's the 'easy' option."

"I'll never be martyred; never can a cat join the kingdom of wolves. I just want to help."

"I... Well..."

Defeated at his own speech games, Edgar agreed to have the molluskan tag along, an ever watchful sage lurking in his footsteps.

"How deep has she gone?"

"As far as Wellington can run, I'd assume," he dimly replied. "If memory serves me correctly, we're under uptown now; circumvented Zest entirely."

Kat was determined, too willing to lose herself. Even so, she wasn't lost to Edgar. Talking down danger was a speciality of his; another trait adopted from dear old daddy.

"Your kindness is unlike that of any man I've ever met," Opyus said slowly. "It makes me wonder–"

"I can hear her," Edgar interrupted. "This way."

They walked into an open tube, with a sluice, slightly agape from its base, blocking the way ahead. A disgruntled Kat held her blade to Wellington's throat, as the pair struggled beside the sluice. Still wearing Beth's face, now doused in sweat, she gritted her teeth, and towered over the downed brute, mocking his impending doom.

Sensing her instability, Edgar yanked her off Wellington's crumpled body as the once proud Master lay there, defenceless. They struggled for a moment – Kat grappled in and out of his hold, losing her blade under the sluice.

"Back off, yuppie. I need to end this!" she yelled, fighting the inevitable.

"Ending this doesn't need to involve another death." Edgar stayed firmly between Kat and her nemesis.

"Svanold to the rescue," Wellington murmured from the ground. "The betrayer, hoping to become the redeemer. How original." The air of friendship he'd slipped under Wellington's nose was now gone, and only the stench of a traitor lingered. "Heads will roll for this, all your miserable heads."

"You're in no position to make aggressive gestures," Opyus said.

"And Svanold isn't ready to reason with this monster of a women," Wellington replied. "She'll kill him just to get to me."

"She would not," Edgar denied.

"You sure?" Kat said, begging him to call her lethal bluff. She stepped up to him, pressing their foreheads together, and whispered in his ear. "You have no idea what I would do."

He felt a compression like never before, with doubters on both sides. His worries about self-preservation became all the more real.

"This is why I hate people. All you do is yell and throw your weight around like angry toddlers. And in the end, it gets you nothing. That is why I'm protecting both of you, because I see a better way," he moaned.

"There's no other way," claimed Wellington, convinced in his pessimistic ways.

"Really? Well, prepared to be enlightened, Ryon."

Kat disagreed. She pulled Edgar aside, and prepared to strike down Ryon for a third time.

"Or... I could end this swiftly," she offered.

"This lesson applies to you too. The world could use two fewer activists." Granting him room to breathe, Kat backed down, allowing a moment of reason to shine though. "Most people love to use the example of 'kill or be killed': two options, and two options alone. But can't you just talk or walk too? Is that so hard?"

"Please… talking, really?" Wellington said. "Weak men lose their hearts to talking, and I'll never make that mistake again. I lost my wife to words."

"And I lost my husband the day I walked away," added Kat. And in that last exchange, Kat's face dimmed and realisation struck. Its nature was unknown, but any change in this heated situation was welcome.

As for his own warmth, Edgar's voice became harsh, and sorrow battled fury for a turn to speak. In the end, both took the floor in a ray of despair.

"No, you lost those close to you because you walked and talked too late. I'm not recommending we hash out a treaty, kiss and make up. All I long for is one night where the good and bad guys just leave well enough alone! When you fight, and it's already too late. You lose, regardless of the outcome."

It was a simple premise that he'd tried pitching to many people over the years, all falling on deaf ears. But now it had finally stuck in someone's mind, though not the one he expected.

"He's right," agreed Opyus. "This can end with the tune of peace in our hearts. Far more desirable than the drumbeat of war, don't you think?"

"You're falling for this? You can't possibly want to keep an emotionless killer like Wellington alive." Kat was losing ground, and with it came an erosion of will.

"No, I don't. But with half the High Council already missing, the Order would cease to function if it had any more absentees. And as religious man, I can't let the wheels fall off faith's wagon again," Opyus said, trying to open her eyes to the bigger picture.

"I'm not asking for defeat, all I want is one moment of mercy," Edgar added. "Do what *he* can't."

Kat's willpower faltered over time, and she swapped out her aggression for the soft embrace of realisation.

"I can't," she said, fighting to keep her old code intact. Her words took on a wetness to them, and felt weighted with emotion.

"The path of the damned is a hard one to follow. I promised Catherine to save you. If you choose to follow this path, I can't keep that promise." Edgar grabbed her by the arm, firmer than his stand. "Do this for her, not me."

A sister's love was unconditional, and that didn't always mean positive things. If misusing love could ward off hate, Edgar held no qualms about his actions.

"And if it was your loved one that Wellington butchered? Could you bear the loss?"

"I've already lost someone close to me. Beth isn't an ex–but she damn well doesn't love me right now," Edgar admitted. The perfect face of his beloved wife surfaced, causing a wave of depression to drown out his hope-filled smile.

Kat paused. "I'm sorry. I didn't think..."

"It's alright; most don't. She was funny and kind, a little harsh sometimes, but I loved her for it. That was until I introduced her to the Order: to a life of combat over comfort. Now she's become a different person entirely, and I haven't seen her in such a long time."

Beth had carved a hole into his heart that wasn't easy to fill, but with enough time, he hoped to return one day. Return to her and return to paradise. As his father used to say: the road to paradise was paved with good deeds.

"If you lost your wife to the Order, then you must want to avenge her. Why not just let me end this vendetta and be done?" Kat asked, countering against his persistent argument.

"We moved on. May a bad past not dictate a bad future," Opyus said, passing on sage advice to the pair.

"No. I never do, 'move on'. I never look back on yesterday; just run head-first into tomorrow," Edgar confirmed. "If Ryon dies today, it'll be awfully difficult to run into tomorrow as the Order falls to chaos. This act of kindness, Kat, it may seem small, but has a long lasting effect. Please.. please just be kind, for the people of the Vitalands... for Zarp, for Beth, the Goddess. For me."

Kat heard his admission, his humanity, and crumpled before him.

"I'm sorry." It was all she said, but was enough. An admission of her own.

"Don't apologise; you're a good soul," Edgar said, "But now, Kat, now we run."

He moved back the way they came, full of power after his verbal bout was won; a victor's feast of satisfaction.

"Where in the hell do you think you're all going?!" roared Wellington, standing upright. "You need to answer for this… this… sin!"

"It's over, Ryon. Back down," Edgar replied, preaching solid advice.

"I never back down. You won't kill me, and I'm too weak to bring about your own end." The Battlemaster was clutching a chest of broken ribs, but still talked so deeply. "I can still follow you to the edge of Magnus. If it's a stalemate you want, I'm more than 'appy to oblige."

Never had Edgar anticipated such dedication on Wellington's part. The Order followed its master, and if the master was to follow them? Carnage would trail them on a short leash. Wellington sensed his unease. "The Order's might will not fall to you, Ed. Not today."

"Guess again." Opyus said, rallying next to the mayor.

"What would you do to me, Kraken? You had quite the reputation, back home. The killer of kindness, reduced to Eddy's pet goldfish. A pathetic path for a warrior to weather."

"Yes, evidently I need to evolve my tactics." Opyus tackled Wellington back to the ground, cracking what ribs remained. "Go! I'll make sure he doesn't follow."

The elderly mercenary would be sacrificing his freedom for them; noble and foolish.

"That's not happening," Edgar protested.

"Don't bother convincing me otherwise, kid. I made up my mind the second you sprung me. The Order will think me a monster no more."

"Let go of me, traitor. I'll fucking end you," yelled Wellington, wrestling the molluskan. But the two were matched, neither besting the other, both waiting for the Order to find them.

"You just made it on to my list of friends, deacon," Edgar said, granting the finest thanks he could. They shared a salute good-bye, and that was it; back to choir.

"That was selfless of him," he said to Kat, "and we won't let that be in vain."

The symmetry was beautiful – Opyus stayed with Wellington to balance their morals, while Edgar accompanied Kat to do the same.

***

Together, Edgar and Kat retraced their movements to jail's pipes and further on, to the mouth of Zest. But when they made it to the exit, the Order was guarding the myriad of piers along Bridgeport's docks.

A ship was missing, which gave Edgar hope, but would leave him alone to care for Kat in the nest of enemies. Babysitting was a task suited more for Zarpadon, but as the crystivine was now sailing Zest, the challenge fell to him.

"There's too many. I can't take 'em all on," Kat stoutly observed.

"Don't worry. It's time for Plan C."

"'C'? What happened to 'B'?"

"Well, B was to leave on another boat, but times have changed. I think we'll go rural for this trip."

Then, Edgar whisked his new partner in crime away. The location? His home away from home. To go forward, he went back. Grabbing Kat by the hand, he guided her through the winding canal until they reached a ladder leading up to a manhole.

"Up and out. If we hurry, we might catch the rest before they head offshore," he instructed, keeping an eye out for any pursuing shock troops.

The manhole opened out onto a street near Bridgeport's northern edge, a very extravagant part of the city, reserved for the rich and famous. Lined by houses of brick, not cobble, and lit by state-of-the-art lanterns – using the light from pyrus rather than whale oil – this place was a pricey privilege.

"This is wonderful. Gaffer once mentioned that all of Midgartt's best actors and playwrights live here," said an awestruck Kat.

"Sounds about right. I've seen more quill jockeys and wordsmiths about these streets than I can count. You like plays?" Edgar asked as they strutted further east.

"No, never had the chance. Most of the company I keep favours arenas to stages."

"Well, when this is all over, I'll personally see to it that you witness one of the finest plays in town. 'Love, Loss and Laughter.'" He'd been longing to see it himself for months now, and Kat made a perfect plus one.

"Sounds good to me," she smiled. "Where are we heading, anyway?"

"Right over there." He pointed to a large manor on the corner of the street.

"Fancy place, Edgar. Who lives here?"

"You answered that yourself. I do. This is where I hang my hat, and this is our way out of Bridgeport."

The two storey home was similar to his attire. The outside was blackened stone, while the interior was glowing brightly through the windows; Edgar did love to colour co-ordinate. Each corner of the building had its own pointed spire on the roof, connected to one another by a flatter design, and the centre was hollow, containing a garden area upon it.

Serene afternoons in the garden soaking in sun, were all that kept him sane these past few years as mayor. Little joy and much less peace lived in the life of a politician.

"You live here? The best place I've stayed is half the greatness of this," Kat complimented him, ogling at the fine architecture.

"It's not the house we're interested in. We're heading for the stables." These were simple compared to the manor, with three pens holding three horses. Each were jet black with glossy manes running down their crests. "Kat, meet Orion, Stella, and Zion," Edgar said, introducing his prized steeds.

"You named them after a fairytale?" Kat raised an eyebrow, judging him ever so subtly.

"Not the fairytale. The real world inspiration for them. Like your molluskan friend, I'm a man of faith." Opening the pen, his horses rushed out to greet him; Stella even paid Kat some mind. "Which one do you want to borrow? Zion is friendly but Stella's got some real power behind her," he said. "I'm taking Orion, so he's off the table."

"Then we ride?"

"Then we ride."

Kat got closer to the horses, and familiarised herself with them, stroking Zion's mane and petting Stella. They were tame, at least around Edgar, decades of training having paid off in his favour.

"I'll ride Stella," she concluded, and mounted the stubborn horse.

Edgar then said his goodbyes to Zion as the two left the stable and the city and made their journey alongside Zest, all in hope of rejoining Zarpadon.

"The reins of the humdrum life are too weak to hold us, Kat. The world's gonna love the mischief we create. After all, this is what I live for: the open road, and a goal far from reach. Gotta love a steep climb." Edgar celebrated by making Orion rear up as they rode off under the rising sun.

Solaris' return from exile was at hand, and his rising star was there to light their path to victory. For each sunrise was just a sign that the best was yet to come.

Chapter 6: Dancing Moonlight

Hart, accompanied by his captain, made haste to Roy's Fork in hopes of chasing down Hunter's entourage.

Since arriving at the Fork, he'd kept the kid on a tight leash, never breaking visual contact, even forfeiting sleep in the process. He was close now, so close to retrieving Kenneth and getting back to the humdrum of life.

Feeling victory in his bones, not even the sweet serenade of sleep could distract him.

"Boss, three days have passed and you've dedicated no time to the pillow. You should sleep," suggested Boyd. It was an attempt to help, but Hart didn't care.

"Hunter's been holding out here for a while now. He's planning something. Why else would he be prolonging the search?" he said. "I want to be present and awake when he makes this all-important move. I've already lost too much to exhaustion before. Never again."

They were camping on the roof of a deserted store, opposite the Fork's inn. Hunter and the other paladins weren't inside, but had a large, makeshift camp set up near the stables. Often travellers would use the itchy confines of a stable-yard as cheap housing. Even babies had been born in that breed of dirt and muck.

Jelz left with Hunter and patrolled the camp with a watchful eye. Hart was a traitor to the Order, and Jelz was no different, choosing to betray his own home rather than his god.

Hart couldn't fault the molluskan for joining Hunter. If the tables were turned, he'd do the same.

"Boyd, be a dear, make a run to the apothecary. I'm fresh out of Sleep-Less," he ordered, seeking a minute of solitude.

Being his ever loyal employee, Boyd departed down the street to fetch more of the stimulating elixir, Sleep-Less.

It was a potion that worked as advertised; Hart slept less, at the cost of discomforting mental anguish. The consequences of the drink meant little, and he marched on with the knowledge of Kenneth's defeat by his side.

While Boyd was gone, he continued to observe the inn and its residents. If Hunter had something planned, then the inn would be where it'd all go down.

Drinkers drank, and singers sang – nothing piqued an interest. But the gods favoured Hart at last by making a familiar face apparent in the crowded inn: that of Ash Belwert. He hadn't seen the dwarf in some time, but still recognised that face, albeit warped by scar tissue and the unfashionable elf ear grafted to it.

"Son of a whore," Hart whispered, pulling out a monocular for a closer inspection.

Ash wasn't alone. He was followed by two other freaks and a woman wearing lilac robes. They drew many queer looks, especially the beast that lay beside them – a monster of meat and malice.

"What in Bethany's name is he doing?" Hart said, as he focused on robed leader. Her frizzy brown hair covered an amulet made of copper, one he'd been offered once upon a time, back when he'd first met Madame Osiris – to whom the girl held a familial resemblance.

If the raggedy Osiris was involved with Ash, then the elf ear could mean the return of a certain witness: another weed to rip from Magnus' soil. "Donsis, you feculent speck of luck. I best save a shot for you."

Using the cooling late-night air to steady his mind and think, Hart turned to the future. With Ash's arrival changing his operation for the worse, the needed to adapt arose.

The cultists didn't distract him for long, as Hunter and a small group of personal protection entered the inn from the side; boozed determination covered the stumbling hunter all over. Moving straight towards Ash's table, worry struck Hart, dreading to think what would happen to the undead squad if Hunter also spied Belwert amongst the crowd.

"Let's see how this plays out. I doubt Hunter could pick him out. All skill, no substance, that Hunter."

True to form, Hunter pushed straight past Ash to reach a table at the far end of the room. Sitting at it was a young woman, barely out of adolescence, with wavy, black hair that covered her face, only showing a pair of wide, dark eyes. The hair continued to her hips, wrapping gently over her ill-fitting sweater. The black outfit sagged over her hands, obscuring them, and was used as a dress to cover her ripped tights.

Hunter sat by her, blabbering on about something just out of reach. She didn't take well to Hunter's words, and doused him with a drink before heading upstairs, leaving the boy with dampened spirits and clothes.

"What an ass. Right, Warden?" observed a foreign voice with great bombast. The intruder's words bled class. He was no stranger to speaking, with a thick Vitalands accent, pronounced with depth and regular pauses.

However, the bass-heavy words were tainted with the shimmering reflections of a dozen other tongues – Castern, Karinese, Wastern, the list went on. The intruder was learned, but a traveller, with nowhere to call his home.

"Can I help you?" Hart asked, keeping his gaze on Hunter.

The clopping of metal-heeled boots chimed from behind as the intruder came closer. An air of cinnamon and several other unknown spices joined the clopping. 'Fragrant men are weak men' – he'd been taught this while serving in the Wastern military, and this intruder was going to be no different.

"It's customary to face a man of higher rank. And you'd do well to learn my visage."

Humouring the spice-scented man, Hart turned to face his supposed 'superior', only to find an older gentlemen smirking with his arms open. One arm of note was plated with a creaking, dull gauntlet. Looking like a noble in a black suit, the gentleman approached at a slow pace, bowed graciously, and introduced himself. "Percival, a pleasure to meet you. I've been waiting for this reunion longer than you could fathom. I'm Kalsec. Charmed."

Kalsec stood parallel to him, keeping a curled smile on his sickly face. This did feel like a trap, but then that was what the best traps felt like: safety.

Circular scars and black veins hidden by bad make-up were clear under the moon's glow, and what couldn't be seen was wrapped under the tight, white collar of Kalsec's shirt. Beside his pale face were flowing strands of long silky hair, dark as the night sky but with the sheen of the sun.

"Proceed, Sir." Displaying a sheathed blade, Hart heard Kalsec out.

"Wonderful. You can never fathom how much it pleases me when I see a man live up to his reputation."

"I have a reputation?"

"Percival Hart, a broken fiddle whose tune is nothing but a recital of my own melody."

Hart bridled at the comparison. "Calling us similar is an unwise thing to do. I've killed before, have you?"

Lifting aside his jacket, Kalsec revealed a silver sabre unlike anything crafted locally. The handle's guard was shaped in a diagonal cross, leading down to a single-edged beauty sharper than Kalsec's vocal wit. Moonlight hit the straight sabre, forcing the blade to take on a pure white appearance. Blindingly majestic, the thin sabre was nothing to trifle with; even a sore-eyed Hart could tell it was partly illethium.

“Oh, Warden, you and I weep with the same honours; broken soldiers who seek war in the hunt,” replied Kalsec. “If I preferred the sword to the sheath, I dare say I'd relish in your company. But alas, my heart is destined for a far greener pasture.”

“What are you doing here, Kalsec? Even if you’re my supposed 'superior', you have reason to stalk me.” Hart was intrigued by the deathly man, and maybe even entertained a degree of admiration, for their composition was admittedly parallel.

“You can call this a stab in the dark, or simply put, careful placement of luck. Take your pick. The reason for my arrival is mysterious as my title, I can assure you this,” Kalsec joyfully proclaimed. “The Shadow, the Moondancer, Holy Blade of the Lost Concort: all titles I've been granted, but never quite earned. Still, I prefer my original calling, given by my true master. World, my name is Kalsec!”

With this prideful gesture, his arms opened further, and he flung his hands to the air, parading the title to the world of docile chaos around them. It was sickeningly inspiring to watch such a pragmatic danger.

“And 'Kalsec', is that a real name?” Hart asked.

First impressions meant the world to a soldier; key to figuring friend from enemy. So far, quite the impression was made in both directions.

“Far from it. My real name is lost to time, holding little meaning, even to my father.”

“A sad tale, but distractions of that nature don't work on me. Why are you here?”

Lowering his arms, the gent stepped to the edge of the building, averting his gaze to the inn.

“Why, I here for the same guttersnipe as you.”

Another admirable goal, but Hunter wasn't a delicacy to be shared, and Hart neglected the honour amongst fiends.

“That's not happening. Hunter is my target,” he replied plainly.

“Hardy. I've longed for the boy for longer than you. If we work together–”

“I could kill you,” Hart relentlessly warned. “But respect my wishes, answer me correctly, and you may live to see the sunrise.”

“Never have I held any love for the sun. It hurts my eyes more than anything,” said Kalsec. He backed away, but didn't back down. “But you! You can’t get enough of it. For it was the sun that liberated you from the horrors of Kenneth Porter, another man with a mangy reputation.”

How he knew Kenneth's name was unbeknownst to Hart, a curiosity that had to be addressed.

"You know me better than anyone still breathing-"

"I don't breathe. Not as necessity, anyway," Kalsec interrupted. "But please, gone on."

"-but why bother to accomplish such an empty feat? Knowing me is a pointless study."

"I've had more spare time in my life than you'll ever want. It was only right to dedicate some of that time to my mirrored tragedy."

"My very own shadow..." Hart sarcastically concluded.

"Exactly. Now, we have to settle whatever bad beginnings we just fought through; to unite and finish Hunter together. This will be my last offer," Kalsec boldly said, offering another hand in partnership.

Hart wasn't looking to share revenge with this stranger, even if Kalsec was his shadow, it was his duty alone to stop Hunter, a burden that'd follow in pursuit of Kenneth. Pushing away the friendly hand, the Warden cast off the offer.

"Like I said, I'm not sharing."

Without a hint of anger, Kalsec met the declination with a passive sneer.

"Shameful display of showmanship, Percival. Kenneth may survive you yet. Tell me, how do plan on besting Hunter's thick guard? The boy has a regiment thirty strong, all aching to fight."

"Allow me to worry about numbers. I doubt you'd fare much better than I."

Sneering again, this time with sadism laced throughout, Kalsec pulled his right arm forward, placing it between them. Grasping the kukri's handle, the uneasy warden readied for an attack.

"The old adage 'a house halved is doomed to die divided' applies to the Order. Each section of the sect has its ideals varying from the last; never a unified force. All it takes is one *snap* to truly end the might of this conglomerate."

Snapping his fingers together, Kalsec maniacally chuckled, and the bells of the Citadel tolled in strings of five. Each echoed all the way from Valordolt – their song was deep and rang a patriotic tune, causing the chaos within to lose its docile nature.

The paladins camping below soon struggled to do their duty, clasping their helmed heads in pain, before losing personality; slowly, the knights became puppets possessed. Wasting no time, the knights drew swords against Hunter's loyal guards; an army of thirty became two armies of ten and twenty.

Slaughter happened, strength fought speed, iron fought leather, knights fought hunters. Amidst the carnage, Jelz pulled his fishing pole, and took arms against Lud, and his paladins.

The streets of the Fork became a panicked seed bed, growing screams and blood, all in an effort to slay one boy. Kalsec's tricks were a marvel of mania.

"I'm sorry, Warden. I assume you'll lose a few of your men tonight," Kalsec unsympathetically apologised. Without pause, he grabbed the rifle Hart once held close, lined up a shot in mere seconds, and pulled the rusty trigger. Ricocheting from wall to wall, the bullet soon found a home, nested deep in Hunter's spine, just above the tail bone.

"Worthless snatcher! He was mine!" Hart roared, desperate to save his men. Pulling his kukri on the stranger was easier than he'd hoped. The simplicity of combat seeped into his life once more.

Kalsec's reaction turned to anger. Though being older than most, he grappled Hart's neck with one hand, lifting the warden high into the air. The gentleman held a strength unknown to any other of such outward appearance, and seized the kukri from his grasp, throwing it to the streets.

With a few rasps of air in his lungs, Hart sparingly cursed, "Freak of nature..."

"Naturally," replied Kalsec, dropping him where they stood, "but freaks generate results. Men of raw talent, shunned by the rest of Magnus. Belittled for their greatness. I will end as a giant. And you, Warden, will die a pygmy."

Putting everything into one motion, Kalsec drew his sabre, soaked in the moon, and plunged it down, fast and carefree. Hart closed his eyes, accepting of all that was, and all that would be – the end was near. Life flashed before him: Anya, the kids, and the man who stole them all witnessed his death. But death decided to retreat.

A single, meek gunshot filled the air, drowning the battle below. Boyd had returned, and withdrew the peashooter from his shaking sleeve. That one bullet found home in Kalsec's chest; it caused a stagger, and the sabre narrowly missed.

Harbouring a single graze to the face, Hart survived the stab that was destined for more. Kalsec stumbled with a loss for balance, and fell from the roof, with his sabre in hand.

"Sorry I'm late, boss. The store was out of Sleep-Less," Boyd said, still shaking.

"Better late than never," Hart replied, standing up and examining the deep gash. "Could have been a little quicker though. Almost lost an eye."

"Sorry, boss."

"But good job, Captain. Now, let's finish this."

The war below wasn't in favour of the hunters. Even with Jelz on their side, the numbers were not, and the paladins soon reduced them to two: Jelz and the wounded Hunter.

Things only worsened as a lullaby swept the field; no doubt another trick spawned by Kalsec. The song was childish, but roused the spirits of the cowardly civilians of the Fork, and they too joined the battle.

"A nursery rhyme; but why?"

"I don't care. There's innocents at stake now. Get moving!" the Warden ordered.

He dropped with Boyd behind, lamenting his actions as he cut down his own men, all in effort to save Hunter for himself. The knights were possessed by the tolling bells, unaware of the betrayal, and hopes rose that the bells would end alongside their deaths. The bells only rang faster, supplemented by a louder lullaby.

Kalsec wasn't dead either. Boyd's shot had made the gentleman limp, turning his lung to useless meat, but it wasn't enough. Wheezing and coughing, Kalsec moved towards the inn where Hunter suffered.

The boy was bleeding profusely and had lost control of his legs, but was still screaming, rallying his hunters – a desperate call to the dead. Hunter crawled into the street and saw Kalsec slowly approach.

"You..." gasped the pale boy.

"Hello, my little fledgling. What a pleasure it is to meet again."

Acting as both Hunter's sword and shield, Hart and the captains surrounded the boy, all willing to the very last.

Retaliating immediately, Kalsec stepped away, whistling for the knights, treating them as equals to livestock. Lud and five others formed a barrier around him, each burly suit of armour covering every angle of attack. Their weapons defensively curled around his bloody suit, with Lud's blade situated above the head.

Behind a wall of flesh and iron, Kalsec was happily situated. "My commendations, Warden. Few can hold their own against order like this," he coughed, ever keen to dish out pleasantries.

"I have a supposed reputation to uphold."

"*And* you've managed to ruin my attire." Kalsec added.

"A damn shame. I'll weep for it later."

Hunter tugged at his ankle, choking on words forced through the a bloody mouth.

"Leave me, Percy. There's no point dying for me."

If Hunter believed goodness was what kept them together, the fool was mistaken. A light kick to the downed hunter silenced him from displaying any more wasted affection. Lowering the tip of his blade to the earth, Hart drew a line the dirt road between the two factions.

"This is the line. Step over it, and you're a dead man," he threatened, gambling on the fleeting will of a dying Kalsec.

"Worse attempts have been made to break me," replied the Moondancer, "but you should be the one to fear this line."

The mark in the earth was a symbol of balance, with knights on one side, weighted against the outlaws on the other. Behind Kalsec was Valordolt, sitting pretty behind Vita's tree line, bells and all. Behind Hart and his captains were the wilds, which were unkempt and an awful place to run should the balance become interrupted.

"You aren't looking too good," Jelz said to Kalsec. "That lung looks mighty collapsed."

"Yes, it does. My blackened blood isn't going to be staunched anytime soon," wheezed Kalsec, in a faint reply.

Gently grabbing Lud's bloody blade, Kalsec lowered it, licking the sharp edge and slurping up the crimson that coated it. "Ahh, much better. The refreshing taste of the end. I wonder how yours will taste?"

"I'll admit, that's kinda creepy," whispered Jelz.

"All a tactic: a weak one, coming from a man with a breathing shield of iron men," Hart reassured. "Cross the line, Kalsec. Then I'll see what you're worth."

Replying with a smirk, Kalsec lowered the knight's weapons and stepped away from their hold.

"How's this for cowardice?" He took another step. "You want me to cross the line? Then so be it. After all, you said to follow your orders, Percival."

A man without fear, Kalsec crossed the line. Hart, chilled to the core, bargained for Lud's life before meeting Kalsec's challenge.

"Let my men go, stop the bloodshed, and I'll give you Hunter," he said in trembled words.

"Hunter's mine, whatever the outcome. My bullet pierced him deep. From here on in, this is all for kicks."

Another battle didn't commence, and with super-human speed, Kalsec darted around the four, marking them each with a prick from his sabre. Light and painless was the jab, but it was made with intricate grace and flashes of teal and pink.

Hart and Jelz swung for the suited attacker, but missed. When they recovered, Kalsec was back in the bosom of the possessed – cradled in might.

"And now it begins," Kalsec stated, before hobbling away into the darkness, grabbing his chest.

"Wait! We need to end this," Hart called. "Fight me, man to man."

"Then what would you do, assuming you'd win? Chase a goose around Karin?"

"Yes. All for revenge."

"Revenge? But what of? Is it no longer for *her*?" retorted Kalsec, stumbling further from the line, from the balance he'd put in place. "Ta ta, Warden. May you find peace in this warring world."

Hart had argued that idea years ago; it stopped being for Anya back when she was buried, along with his love. Stumped and bewildered, a reply didn't follow. Kalsec was quick to celebrate, leaving the Fork and diving into the darkness of night. "Exactly what I thought! It's already over, Warden. I've won this battle. Take them, boys!"

Lud and the others didn't leave, but marched toward Hart and his friends, holding a dead look in their eyes. With his enemy gone, all that remained were his friends, his soldiers. Each was willing to kill their warden to the tune of Valordolt's bells.

"Lud, it's over. Lay down your arms," Hart pleaded.

The knights didn't answer, still entranced by the fading bells.

"We can't kill them, boss, they're our own," Boyd fretted.

"We can, we will," Hart ordered, meeting the paladins head on.

This last stand was met with terrible noise, grunts of knights and outlaws, screams of spectating civilians, the distant laughter of Kalsec, and lastly the last chime of the bells. Hart ran Lud through the gizzard upon that final chime, as Kalsec's spell finally broke and the knights returned to the waking world, if only for their final breaths.

"Warden?" Lud said, confused, as death took the brute.

Slaying those loyal to you was a sin, and one that stuck to Hart with ferocity, more than Kalsec's spiteful japes. If the bells had rung once less, then Lud would've lived to serve another day. But, like most of life's actions, it was never so fair.

"They're dead," Boyd sadly realised, in the last moment of the fight.

"We killed them. There's a sick difference," added Jelz.

"Good job… *men*," Hart groaned, before the grip of sleep claimed his tired bones.

***

A whole four hours passed before Hart could be woken, and when he did, he found no one but Jelz to greet him. He'd not been moved from the road, and lay amongst many corpse-less bloodstains; his brothers in arms were all moved, loaded onto carts, ready to be buried.

The graze upon his face itched, and remained as one more battle scar – another regretful war story.

"You look like hell," he said to Jelz, who was covered in all manner of grime.

"You should see Hunter. The priest said he's not gonna make it."

Hart felt no sorrow over this news. Hunter was going to be a burden now anyway, and he was tired of burdens.

"Why not? Lost too much blood?" he asked, so as to not seem overly heartless.

Jelz shook his head. "If only. The healing prayers just aren't working."

This sparked an iota of happiness and wasn't just luck, it was the will of the goddess on Hart's side. He was destined to make it to Kenneth, free of religious or moral shackles.

"Well, when it's your time, it's your time. Anyone else make it?"

"Me, Boyd, and our cleric, Elise. She hid from the skirmish, used the stables as a haven."

"Smart girl. Wish I'd done the same"

"Don't say that, you've done good today," comforted Jelz. "Saving three is better than none."

"Lud might disagree."

"I don't give a damn, Lud can't judge us now. Look... *boss*, we need you, now more than ever."

Even in defeat, people rallied to him. It was an unwise move on all accounts, but a mistake Hart was hesitant to correct. Sole soldiers could win wars of attrition, and he needed the pieces of the broken watchers. The battle was lost, but if Kenneth still breathed, the war still raged.

"Right then, first order of business: Ash. Have you seen a freaky-looking dwarf with an odd ear stitched to his crown?"

"No, boss, I was stuck out in the cold all night; most of us were."

"Dammit! We'll have to chase him down another day. We'll rest for now, save our pain till the sunrise."

"But Kalsec's still–"

"He won't be a problem come morning. Shadows hate the sun."

Before light broke, Hart took a minute to pray for the lost. The black magic of the bells was new, and a dangerous force it was. Regardless of their malleable allegiance, Lud and his men had fought well and honourably, all deserving passage to Etheriam. But Hart wasn't so sure he'd join them one day.

Chapter 7: Ocean of Green

Harlan slept a painful sleep. His body clung to life as a shaky mess, while his mind was subject to a violent onslaught of nightmares; the pleasantry of living near death.

In these dreams, his body was constantly dissolving at the seams as he was washed away in waves of nauseating green waste.

No matter how bad it felt, he persevered, unwilling to drown in the all-dissolving sea. Immediate worries turned to Lucille and Travis – he couldn't leave them wounded and alone on Magnus while he rested in the afterlife. Pride was fleeting in himself, but what remained fought for the wound – his friends.

Persistence paid off, and after what seemed like an eternity, he awoke in a safe embrace. A tent that reeked of odorous medicines mixed with the distinct smell of burned flesh greeted the dwarf. It was an unappealing setting, but calm, with the sun's glow beaming in red hues through the tent's thin canopy.

Looking down at his chest, he noticed that the fleshy wounds were brimming with a thick, yellow paste. Tinted the colour of marigolds, the nose-burning paste relieved the nauseous warmth of his injuries.

To his left was Travis, still sleeping, still fighting. A bloody rag covered his stump, stuffed with a mix of plants and salts meant to clot the blood.

He'd seen a bloated fill of amputees in former days, and Travis was taking it better than all those before him. The boy wriggled around in a dream state similar to his; living a faux nightmare to avoid the real one taking place in the tent.

"Keep on keeping on, Travis," Harlan encouraged, before retracting his view from the cleric's suffering.

Not much else caught his sunken eyes in the sparsely-furnished tent, save for an empty chair seating Lucille's bow and a pestle-less mortar full of marigold mush.

It was easy to be warmed by the idea of Lucille sitting at his bedside, watching over him; a small reprieve from his torment. Trying to stand was fruitless, but he could manage to raise himself upright. All further movements were met with sharp stabs across his flayed body.

"Anyone out there?" he called. "I really need a piss."

A few seconds later, his call was answered, and Haruka pulled back the tent's opening, carrying a plethora of items, including an empty bucket.

"Here," she said, throwing it at his feet.

He looked at it, and back to Haruka.

"What, piss in that?"

"Unless you can stand up," she replied. "C'mon, five hundred years and you've never used a bucket as a privy?"

"Not since the Great War. But back then, everything was used as a privy." Anything but a chamber pot or outhouse wouldn't serve as adequate. Buckets were far too crude, and so he decided to wait. "Think I'll hold out for now. I'm used to the finer things in life."

"Suit yourself then," Haruka said, mixing up more yellow paste in the mortar, violently grinding some added herbs into goo.

"Where are we?" he asked, lying down to dull the pain.

"Declandale. Thomas and Hericore carried the wounded here, and trust me there were a lot of wounded."

"Are the others–"

"They're fine. Aside from cuts and burns, we're all coping. It was you and Travis that scared us," she answered, before even hearing his morbid question. "Meanwhile I got busy saving your lives."

She kept grinding, keeping her gaze away from Travis' stump. But try as she might, the smell of rare meat was inescapable.

"How'd you manage that? I thought killing was your field of expertise," Harlan joked.

She didn't seem impressed with his brand of humour.

"I don't think too much about killing. If you spend too much time pondering the ins and outs of something, you're doomed to forge an interested in it, maybe even enjoy it. It's dangerous to gain an interest in murder."

"Okay, no need to elaborate. What I said was in bad taste," he quickly apologised. "For the record, I don't get a thrill from killing, either. Another bad habit that died long ago."

"Could have fooled me. Donsis seemed like an interest."

Valordolt was far away, and for Harlan this was more than a physical meaning, but one of his memories too.

"What happened with Donsis wasn't interest or passion, it was a mistake."

"Bad taste, right?" She knelt between him and Travis, scooped up a handful of sickly yellow, and started rubbing deep into their burns.

"Careful now. That stings like a cluster of bees."

"A *swarm* of bees," she corrected, putting his wizened knowledge to the test.

"Never called them that back in the day," he lied.

Haruka almost smiled. "Clever excuse. I'm still right though."

Her friendliness increased, as did her carelessness.

"Ouch! That didn't feel very medicinal," he snapped. The numbing pain did indeed carry a sting, but immediately gave way to a cooling salve.

"Sorry. This was Lucille's job until now. I'm still learning the ropes."

"Lu was caring for me?" he replied in a high-pitched squeak.

"Yep. You have Lucille to thank for this too." She held up a glob of paste, reeking worse than Travis. "I knew what the poison was, but she knew of a remedy to counter it. Called this stuff Moris Pâté, a recipe from her home. Only the scars will remain."

"Can't say the same for him."

"We did everything possible. But miracles were his department."

Travis swirled in place, and mumbled chants in his sleep. What seemed like gibberish could easily be some foreign code. The cleric's groans of agony continued for some minutes as Haruka rubbed him down. The same words were yammered over and over: `the wicked rest, but the heroes sleep. The wicked rest, but the heroes sleep'.

"Lucille thinks he's a goner," Haruka said, with doubt.

"And you think otherwise?"

"I *want* otherwise."

For a killer, Haruka had a depth of care for Travis. The young cleric did have a certain sense of kindness about him that was too often redacted in most people, Haruka being a prime example. The girl was caring, not kind.

"Still, you saved me from the grave; that's a step in the right direction," Harlan said, staying positive, "Lucille can be wrong."

"Don't let her hear that. Very proud, that girl."

This bonding felt nice. Haruka wasn't a talker, and he expected her bedside manner to rival that of a depressed troll; how wrong he was. "You and Travis have some sturdy hearts. Those bannasites have a poison that burns through your flesh and taints your blood directly: nasty stuff that can kill in one blow."

"You've used it before?"

"Twice. The second guy survived. That's why I'm here," she admitted, sounding ashamed of the hefty mistake.

"Everyone has their bad days. Like today." Reinforcing this, Harlan clutched at his side as the burns continued to wail for aid.

"It looked like you chose this fate. I saw you take that dive for Lucille."

Heroics were long lost on Harlan – many seemed to forego his good and fabricate the bad.

"Oh, you did?" he replied, nervously waiting for her opinion.

"It was nice. More than anyone has done for me," she thanked. "Good job."

"A compliment? Very out of character. Break it to me fast, Dr Katowa – I'm dying right now, aren't I?" he asked with playful idiocy.

Haruka was quick to roll her eyes. "Keep joking and you will be."

"I can see why Lu enjoys your company. You two are rather alike," he said, "minus the murder debacle, of course."

"I could say the same to you. Wouldn't have though Lu would hold a soft spot for someone of your… uniqueness."

Harlan never assumed others knew of his attraction, but Haruka proved this assumption false.

"Guess I wasn't as inconspicuous as I thought."

"You're the epitome of conspicuous."

"So, you think I have a shot with her?"

Desperation grew over time, when an obsession was suppressed, and the need for a second opinion became vital – a sign that his obsession wasn't overly insane. Haruka gave him a doubtful look, but eventually answered, half-heartedly, "Yes."

"Knew it," he cheered with a grin, taking a breather. His heart may be aching – but this time, love wasn't the culprit.

***

Time passed, and the day did too. When the next began, Harlan, fuelled by the adrenaline of love, pulled himself up and out of the tiny tent into the warm, Karin sun. It was rising on the horizon, and its orange glow engulfed the eastern face of the town. The horizon itself was empty, containing rocky formations and sands reflecting the sun's vibrant orange.

This land was home for many years, and the familiar setting struck him as bleak over the years. His time in the floral landscape of the Vitalands may have ruined the beguiling feeling of home; a tragic part of a vagabond's life.

Even days after the bannasite attack, most of the team were busy resting. The journey was draining of vigour, and Harlan found little reward left in forging on. Really, it was the people who piqued his interests now, not the ideals of heroism.

Though Hericore and Rangar's scales had spared them flesh-scorching acid burns, the two still slept as guardians outside the medical tent. Helena, after fighting to stay awake to watch over her friend's recovery had succumbed to the lure of the dream world, finding comfort tucked up by the tent's mouth. Kenneth was the only one awake.

An increasing mystery, Kenneth was sparring by himself on a sandy plateau, lining up with the sunrise over the town. The fisherman looked heavy with fatigue, and regularly licked his cracked lips in thirst. The desert took the fluid right out of the uninitiated, and Kenneth was the very definition of uninitiated. Creeping over, Harlan surprised the preoccupied fisherman with a 'boo'.

“Whatheshit!” yelled a shocked Kenneth, throwing his priceless sword across the sands, only to retrieve instantly like it was made of glass.

“Relax, it's me,” Harlan said calmly. “That was quite the reaction. Expecting someone else?”

From what he could figure, Kenneth had accrued a legendary status in the world for something infamous. What this was remained enigmatic, but most pride-driven knights seeking a title only need a foe's status, not their story.

“I've been a wee bit jumpy as of late,” the old man confessed.

“Been there,” Harlan related, “like something's peering over my shoulders.”

Kenneth made this admission while retrieving his blade. A simple task? If only. The local wildlife decided to spice things up, and a tiny scorpion with a stinger twice its size crawled over the illethium artefact. The fisherman made many reaches for the sword, only to be warned away by the stinger. How the old man managed to brave Magnus this long was beyond question. Knuckling down and facing the pest, Kenneth ripped the blade from the ground, faster than the scorpion could stab. The creature was cast off into the sand, and scuttled away.

Harlan gazed upon the fisherman, who looked back with dead eyes. The old man was distracted, standing perfectly still, with his blade planted in the sand; occasionally he'd look to the left, but with no lucid intent. He was spaced out, busy listening to an old conversation or one that never happened.

"Hey, Kenneth, you in there?" Harlan continued. Asking a second time with a snap of the fingers, a reply slowly formed.

"Hmm? Sorry. My mind likes to drift too."

"That comes with age; a thing I'm also plagued by," the dwarf admitted. It was rare, but every few moons he'd lose himself in the body of a younger man – a man beside himself. This man was plump and short like he, only with another title, another life; this was likely a stretch of his past too far gone to hold onto permanently. One day, he'd forget today, and tomorrow, and all days after that. But, for now, he was Harlan Ainsworth; a good man, a man who'd help save the world.

"Us old ones, right?" Kenneth smiled, gazing off to the left. "All we can do is find comfort in the past. Better times for all."

"Try and hold onto those days; it takes the edge off," Harlan recommended, before being chilled by a strange feeling, "hard as that may be."

The feeling of companionship lingered in all men, even when alone. Harlan felt such a sensation, with an invisible presence trying to figure him out: a nearby emptiness was looking upon him and frowning… or at least a space that appeared empty.

"After the bannasites, it's hard not being on edge," replied Kenneth. "Out on the sea, we fisherman have a saying: 'yesterday's breeze will be tomorrow's storm'. I reckon that traitorous knight isn't the last of our problems in this dust bowl."

"A wise observation. But then, it never does truly calm down around here. Merc work has its draws. I worry each stop could be our last."

This was never more prevalent than in their current task. The Golden King was still over a thousand miles away, and already they'd been maimed and had limbs carved away. Making it to the bloated land of Barsameil would prove harder than felling its ruler. However, Kenneth seemed to care little for the mountainous task ahead. Shrugging, he simply took it in stride.

"We keep wandering for a reason."

"Storm's on the way, Ken," Harlan said, admiring both the clear sky and the fisherman's glimmer of positivity, "but who's behind the next breeze?"

His attention shortly turned to the illethium sword that Kenneth now clasped in his right hand, with a bandage on his left; a wound that paled next to Harlan's own.

"Practising with one hand? Takes some patience," he commented.

"Tell me about it. Asked Haruka to teach me some techniques, only she was too busy to even reject my request," Kenneth told him in a disheartened voice. "And people have the gall to call me callous."

"Haruka may seem that way, but deep down, I see another Lucille waiting to happen." Harlan grinned without realising the oddity in his words, but Kenneth made sure to tell him.

"'A Lucille'? Geez, you are obsessed."

"You are not the first person to say that," Harlan proudly admitted.

"I'm no judge. I was married by my fourteenth birthday."

"Things were different back then," the dwarf joked. "Anyway, see you around, Ken. I need to see a man about a fish."

Before he could escape to Hemora's company, the fisherman called out to him with a request similar to the one he'd given Haruka.

"Can you teach me?" Kenneth said, in desperate straits. "Not every day a Great War hero walks by."

With a look of sincerity, Harlan declined. "I was no hero."

"I'd beg to differ," called Lucille's soft voice. She stood atop a mound of sand, holding an armful of wrappings and the parts needed for more pâté. With a relieved look upon her face, she dropped what she was doing and ran over. With a volley sharp pains, he accepted her thankful hug and held a long, smug smile. "A step up from daphnes, aye?"

Though he burned and itched, it all seemed to numb when she was there. In a hundred years he'd never felt so calm; Short Fuse seemed so small now. Maybe change wasn't so hard after all.

Chapter 8: Dog Days

Kenneth watched Harlan walk away as the second person to turn down his needs. In the last week, Xander was all he had to guide him down the warrior's path. The ghostly wood elf was beside him as he spoke with Harlan, and found amusement in the continual disappointment.

"Got to admire their consistency. Maybe Travis can help. He can't *walk away* from such an offer."

"Too soon for the cripple jokes, don't you think?" Kenneth asked, looking down at his own marks. Though small, the burns stung deep, and what followed was even worse: defeat at the hands of Langdon, a kid.

He never knew the knight's age – in fact, nobody knew much about him. Philip picked a note off the melted corpse, charred and illegible, with only a partially melted seal of red wax surviving. The red was key, being the shade of a Caster family – rich men buying Langdon's life.

The Council of the Casterlands was made from the leaders of the province's seven divided lands. From the coastal Belmoria to the Vel-Tora clergy, any orders from these powerful lords were not to be undermined.

The knight wore blue, but carried a contradicting seal. A man of many colours was one without trust, and that's what made the Casterlands so devious: a rainbow land, with a rainbow of lords: deception in shining, silver armour.

"The guy's brother is still stalking around the town. Hiding in plain sight. Does that worry you?" asked Xander.

"After Langdon's lies, I'd be surprised if he even has a brother out here. My worries of a slowly approaching Order are double that of some 'brother.'"

"Because if the Order gets here, only one man can be spearing the party."

Kenneth shuddered. "Don't remind me further. But hey, we're safe for now. So let's walk. We might even find fun in this horseless town." Leaving their Chicardé to soak in the sunlight, the pair explored what Declandale had to offer.

Kenneth had only ever been on Karin sands through their ports, and never felt the true beating heat of the south. For all the sand-swept vistas teeming with foreign life, only one beauty was on his mind. It wasn't the various cacti or the flock of charcoal-black hippogriffs circling above the town, but one of life's simpler pleasures. "I'm gonna need something to quench my thirst. Feeling only a little *slightly* charred."

"There's always the water tower," Xander suggested.

"Long as it's cool, I'd drink cow's piss."

"Well, Thomas is over at the bar. Surely he'd be glad to oblige," giggled the ghost.

"Nice to see being dead hasn't dampened your spirits."

Taking offence to this, Xander stopped moving and placed a judging look upon him.

"Oh, I'm not dead. It'd be proper to say that I'm just having an out of body experience." Kenneth didn't see a lie in Xander's logic, but didn't understand said logic either.

"There's another 'you' waiting in the world? A body?" he said, baffled.

"More of a husk. Left him with a friend, years past. Hopefully I'm still in one piece."

"But... you're a ghost?" Kenneth fumbled.

"Ghosts aren't dead people, ghosts are lost souls. I'm just the first person around to ever lose himself without dying. I'm truly trapped in limbo, living without form."

The more Xander philosophised, the less belief remained in the wildness of the story. Lost and lonely men did love to talk; Kenneth was one of these, only with the pleasure of being, too. Ruminating on the wispy hue of purple that floated around him, Kenneth moved on, with the heat motivating him further than Xander ever could.

The worn dirt path through Declandale's centre had a hundred different prints ingrained into it: horseshoes, boots, paws. This town had seen much in its day. A cultural quilt stitched together from a dozen others, the prints weren't all that was bursting with variety.

Outside a barber's played a wheezing accordion, and past that was the inn and its duo of musicians playing the flute and lute. A few paces beyond these sat a burlesque house, and piano chords were struck within; women danced a coquettish can-can for a few spare roths. None of these tunes attracted him, except for one.

A man as shaggy as a he was played the guitar, slowly and softly. It was a lullaby for the wandering cowboy: a song of a life well-spent. With half his days squandered, Kenneth wondered if the remaining years would hold equal waste.

"An old favourite?" asked Xander. Kenneth replied with only a light frown that cast him back to his youth. The ghost continued regardless. "I get the same, you know. Don't let it vex ya. There's a reason we say life 'passes' us by and not 'fails' us. It's because each day done is another victory. Death is the only great failure, and am I glad to still be around… vaguely speaking."

Fluffed with sentiment and an ounce of wisdom, Xander's words were comforting. As the guitar's notes faded, only their warmth remained.

When they reached the pumps, a burly man with a covered face halted them from drawing water. Allegedly, Declandale was under strict rations of water now the general store had been raided. This became another poorly-worded story that Kenneth lost faith in as time paced on. A more likely version of events is that the burly man worked for the local bar, and wanted to filter business into his own pocket. This strategy didn't bother the fisherman: same drink, different tap, no worries.

"Tibin, I know that's you," said a sleazy voice from across the street. "Go and torment some other newcomer." He saw the grey-coated man from the flats strut to the conflict, head first.

After being gutted, Rick made an impossible recovery at the hands of Declandale's medical staff. It was called a miracle by most, even fooling the seasoned folks like Hemora and Lucille. This was no miracle – the gods were never kind to the common man, experienced first-hand by the abandoned fisherman.

What saved Rick was a trick of dark origin – no question. Alas, the dark arts could never lured Kenneth, and his mind stopped theorising there.

"Piss off, Rick. I ain't taking orders from a stiff like you," replied Tibin.

"I wasn't givin' you an order; merely some advice."

"Wise-guying me ain't so wise. Think you could take me on?" Tibin said, rising to the occasion.

Rick tilted his head to side, clicking his nick in place with a horrid snap. "One of you Caster boys has already tried killing me once. Didn't work out too well. Now move along."

Kenneth, now stuck between two opposing factions in a feud he wanted no part in, skulked away from the fiery contest. But, like all slugs, Tibin slithered away from Rick's threat.

Brimming with salt, a defeated "whatever" left Tibin's mouth, and he left their lives for good.

"Thanks for the help, I guess," Kenneth told Rick. "Nice to see you out soaking in Solaris' bounty."

"Good to be back. Thanks to my friends in the crimson hoods, I'll live to see the week's end," Rick replied, reaching out to pump up some water.

The pump sounded broken, with an elongated groan accompanying each splutter of water. After overuse, the town had ruined the oasis that supported them; ever the siphons of want, Magnus' desires would sire ruin to come. Maybe this was what Hericore fought against: the wasteful want of mortal man.

"With such a recovery, people started calling it a miracle," Kenneth notified him.

"It's bull," Xander said, "I can tell."

"What can I say. I was always strong of faith. Couldn't be luck," Rick said, unable to hear Xander's disbelief.

"I agree," Kenneth said, appealing to both men's replies. "Too convenient for luck."

"I can break off and scout out his shack. Dig up some dirt," offered Xander.

"Say, can you run an errand for me," Rick followed. Answering both with one word, he agreed with a wholehearted 'yes'. "Perfect. I'm meeting up with your drake boss, Hericore. I have an... interesting proposition for him. Philip was my first contact in the group, and help me uncover a break in my investigation. Can you fetch him for me? The old back ain't what it was ever since Langdon."

The Greycoat was a suspicious gent, but with no reason for such negative notions, Kenneth feigned friendship.

"You had me at 'perfect', Rick."

"Great to hear. You should come along too. Be nice to have an older, experienced dome at the meet-up." Kenneth raised a thumb to the idea as he too partook in the refreshing water from the depths of the desert. "Swell. Be seeing you..?" Rick said, awaiting a name from him.

"Kenneth."

"Kenneth, huh? There are worse names."

The detective promptly left for the tents, leaving the fisherman with his apparition ally. It wasn't long until well water filled his gut, and they took off, aiming to retrieve Philip from the soft walls of the Bled Lizard.

"Think you can handle this?" Kenneth asked.

"All I do is spy on people," Xander replied, confidently.

"Beats being alive and never spying on people though. That lack of knowledge is unsettling."

"It's better that way. Every war in history started by someone discovering what should be buried," Xander lectured. "Ignorance is bliss."

"Better to live in peaceful dark, than to die in the light," Kenneth deduced, coining what he believed to be an insightful quote. Unfortunately, he failed to note the pretentious nature of it. Xander did not.

"Calm it on the philosophy, Ken, that's my deal. I know you're getting wise in your old age, but seriously?"

"You're one to talk. Your body must be what, in its sixties by now? The world without Greenhills has lasted 'bout as long as I've drawn breath."

Xander paused before answering, and Kenneth pondered whether the ghost had genuinely forgotten, or if it was too private a thing to ask a formless soul.

"Sixty-three… maybe four."

"So yeah, you're the olden," Kenneth finished.

"Yes, but at least I've learned how to swing a sword in that time."

Kenneth looked indignant. "I'm catching up. This old dog can still learn some new tricks."

"You sure can, old man. Who the hell you talking to?" said a voice to their right.

Horror-stricken, he saw Philip standing in the doorway to the inn. Shirtless and confused, the well-toned lad awaited a definitive response to the revealing question.

His whispers to Xander now heard, Kenneth prayed to the unkind gods for one favour; an act of deception. The time came to put his own lies to the test.

Chapter 9: Crack in the Mask

Philip had a rough night. The smack Langdon landed on him caused more than just a mere headache. Yesterday was the blood leaking from his nose, and now he'd survived a frightful barrage of horrors within his dreams.

Premonitions? No – pure fear was out to kill him. For months, he'd longed for an exciting dream, but this abolished expectation.

Now he wore sweat-filled garments, unbuttoned and shoeless before a rambling Kenneth. Trust was lacking in his head now that Langdon had knocked it clean out, and scepticism took its place.

“Morning, kid. I was just looking for you,” Kenneth said, nonchalantly.

“Brilliant. But that's doesn't answer my question. Now who were you talking to?” Philip asked again, trying hard to sound casually interested.

Kenneth paused before an answer was mustered, forming the already sceptical thoughts into suspicion. Langdon referred to 'other agents' working against Hericore's movement, and right then, Philip wanted to place the boot onto anyone that would fit it.

“I talk to myself, sometimes. Helps clear my head.”

It could be a valid excuse, but then the guise of 'wandering knight' also made a valid excuse. Now, Travis was at Bethany's gates – next time it could be Helena, or worse, Philip’s own life at risk; an unfortunate position to be trapped in.

But again, Hericore's wisdom shone into his sore head, and as if the drake had said the words himself, he let it pass.

“I could stand to clear my head!” Philip said, with a false smile. “Insomnia would be a kindness.”

“And here I thought I was the only one,” replied Kenneth. “I've been asked to summon you to camp.”

Sickness had wrapped Hericore in sloth, and this seemed to worsen after giving a fraction of his life to save the suicidal Rangar. Kindness could kill; kindness had killed. Philip would follow Hericore's words, but never his actions; those were just foolish.

“I'll be back in a minute. Just need to get my shoes, then you can point me to the boss.”

“It's not Hericore that requested you.”

“Then our detective friend is up and about,” Philip concluded, then returned to the Lizard's shade.

He took a generous amount of time to ready himself, valuing appearance over most things, making sure to tame his wild curls and straighten out the creases in his sandy trousers. The black streaks of smoke still lingered on his shirt, and a brown poncho was used to cover the unsightly marks from view, a cheap and stylish solution to the problem. "I'm in a land of overalls, hats, and ponchos. I bought a poncho… good grief."

Ten minutes of preparation later, Philip left the chilled confines alone, being certain not to wake Thomas from his drunken slumber. A bear with a sore head was bad, but a minotaur with one was like hell on Magnus.

"'Bout time. Did you sew that cloak yourself while you were up there?" Kenneth complained, a nice change from the mopey man he'd rescued last week; a sudden change expected from a Ganger, not knowing how Kenneth acted.

The Ganger theory was less than a paranoid rabble in Philip's mind, but still held a seat in the halls of his internal judgement.

"Now that's the kind of Kenny I wanted to see back in Valordolt; all sass, no class. I'm sure your days with Helena made a difference," Philip hoped.

"You found a nice woman. Dangerous when fighting and talking."

Helena was never a strong talking point when conversing – he found her skills commended enough as they were.

Philip smirked. "You should see her in the bedroom. That whip isn't just for the battlefield."

"I was born in the wrong generation," claimed Kenneth, holding a distant admiration for Philip's way of life.

The pleasant talk was wearing thin, and each word came as a struggle. Things kept gnawing inside; the dandy dreamed visions of betrayal. But from who?

The 'fisherman' had changed since Refracted Light much faster than the others. The old man's new attitude perplexed him, soon to consume his thoughts, shifting their talk to a private affair, a choice made for security.

"Let me ask you something, Kenny," Philip asked. "Your crimes. What were they?" All good monsters hid the piles of bodies they'd created. If Kenneth was the next bump in the road, he too would have covered his bodies.

With a groan Kenneth repeated the same spiel from the prison. "I told you. I was innocent."

"Whether you're an innocent or no, it doesn't answer my question."

Reluctantly, Kenneth answered, "Murder."

"Whose murder?"

"You wouldn't know any of them."

"Any of *them*? You're a serial killer? 'Talk of the Regatta Ripper is just a rumour', Hericore told me." Philip loved to mimic other people. It was no surprise – his voice could become grating after so many questions. It was fun to try a new mask on every once in a while.

"Does it matter? You won't know who I'm talking of. Hell, I don't."

"Then you can tell me," Philip persisted.

Kenneth held off the wave of questions until they reached the town's exterior; the old man was masterful at dodging an answer – not that it mattered now.

With a lacking amount of enthusiasm from both parties, they soon brought up the sore subject of Langdon. The traitorous bastard was the least of Philip's concerns now he rested in a shallow grave; the dead were of no consequence. But Kenneth persisted on the topic, determined not to let the sleeping dog lie.

"The kid was a furious, little shit, with anger in every step he took. But you can't deny the furious little shit's swordsmanship. He took on Haruka, Lucille, Hemora, and Rangar at once. The kid even had time to kick my ass the process."

It wasn't hard to imagine someone 'kicking his ass'. Kenneth was a tortured soul, and more importantly, a weak, tortured soul. If push came to shove, Philip believed even he could take on the old man. If his suspicions held any water, he may have to.

"Really? Damn, we could of used him in Yellemette. Would've been one for the songs. 'Langdon the Legend', and all that."

"And now he's dead. At this rate, we'll be joining him," wallowed Kenneth. The fisherman had more vigour when he'd been tied up in Central, showing how much this journey was taking from them.

"You, maybe," Philip conceded. "Me? Not so much."

"You sound confident. If you've got any tips for living a long life, then please, pray tell," the old man commented.

"I have a feeling that I'll be around for a long time. I'm calling it now: I can see myself sitting pretty, years from now." When the premonitions still found him, Philip saw the brilliance of things. One day, the world would be his, the mountains, valleys, and towers. He'd shine under all the stars in the sky. His visions had never been wrong before, and the thought of finally finding paradise was one of few things still warming his heart.

Kenneth sighed. "I wish I had that outlook on life. Since leaving Refracted Light, I feel as if I left myself there." And with that harrowing statement, they finally arrived at camp.

Most of the crew were rising to the glare of the desert sun. Rangar was the only one to stay snoozing under the heat, shielding his face with an arm of scales. The other was no longer in a sling, and only a wooden splint held the cracked bones together.

Helena approached her honey and cuddled up with him. She was worried these days, but refused to say why, instead choosing to hug it out in his arms.

The comfort calmed her hidden anxiety, though Philip could only focus on how much hotter and sweatier it made him, their connection breeding an arid cloud of musk.

"Hey, Plum. Bad night?" he asked her, to which she frowned. Helena rarely frowned – not any more, not for months. "Well, I'm also in that boat. Could be worse, though. Could be Travis."

"Hericore's chalking him up as a loss," Helena replied.

"And Hericore usually doesn't know what he's talking about," Philip quipped back. "Now where is that old, dithering drake?"

"In the crimson tent, watching over Travis. Wants to see you, I think."

"On it now, Plum. Just keep a smile for me, okay?" With resilience, she cracked a tired smile, and kissed him away.

"Good luck, Hun."

"Never needed luck," Philip replied, tapping his forehead. But this cocky action was met with another wave of ache, and as Helena sulked away, he whispered, "Least not before now."

If his window into the future did leave, then things would turn south for his plans in the south, tragically mirroring Hericore's own spiralling downfall. The pressure of a billion lives rested cumbersome on his shoulders, pushing further strain on his tight lungs and weakened heart.

Kenneth followed the kid to the tent's flaps, determined to gain entry into Rick's meeting as well.

"Whoa, Ken, this could be private. You sure boss-bird wants you inside?"

"Rick invited me," answered Kenneth, with confident, soft words. "Plus, I think there's more to him than he lets on."

Philip snapped into action, and his speech picked up pace with a wave of excitement. "You think he's a traitor? Like Langdon?"

"Maybe."

Everyone's motives took a strange turn, warping previous theories. Lesser, cowardly men and drakes would allow this to pass, but Philip capitalised on it by promoting Kenneth's ideas, in the hope it would chip away his mask and reveal the Ripper's face.

"Then I need you, buddy. Now more than ever. We can expose Rick together," he said, trying to win camaraderie.

"Alright, pal," the old man replied slowly. "Never knew you felt the same way. Guess we're in this together."

Like a social play, Philip took on a false role; a new mask, one against Rick, all to absolve the detective of Kenneth's wrongly-founded accusations. It was a strategy that cast a large shadow over anything birthed by Hericore's mind: a ruse to make his beloved proud.

"Okay, let me do the talking. You watch Rick, and take a mental note of anything... dubious or ill-willed," Philip planned.

"Done deal," Kenneth said, sounding more than ready for some sleuthing of his own.

It was a small tent, but it managed to house Hericore's girth, along with Rick and the shivering Travis, deep in recovery. With a look of concern worn without force, Hericore looked upon Philip with open eyes. The drake greeted him, getting straight to the point for once, forgoing any pleasantries.

"Philip, Kenneth. Rick believes he has found the stronghold of the bandit clan that Langdon was in league with," Hericore croaked with concern.

"You say this like it's a bad thing," Philip smiled.

"That's because I now know where, all thanks to your advice. But the location is a terrifying place for a group of murderers to dwell," Rick added.

Interest piqued, Philip's eyes lit up.

"What terrifying place are we talking about?" Words such as 'terrifying' sparked great fires in his brain, flames of interest that he fanned religiously.

"Langdon spoke with his brother while he dragged me out into the flats," said Rick. "Heard mention of a place he called 'the Heart of Declandale'. This can only mean the caverns beneath the town: the source of our water."

"Stealing the town's bottled water, only to control the ground source. Got to hand it to the bandit scum, that's actually a smart move," Philip commended.

"Indeed, but this puts us at a disadvantage," Hericore said, silencing his misplaced admiration.

"With the ability to cut off the town's pump, the bandits have quite the bargaining chip," Rick added.

Another clever move from the unwashed adversaries. Philip pondered the situation for a moment; accounting for all the variables, as Travis shuddered feverishly at his feet.

"Langdon was troubling. Most troubling. What he did to us could've ended our mission in its infancy. Travis saved us, but at what cost?" Hericore ruminated.

The drake had grown ever more depressed over his year of cursed illness, losing all notion of hope with each given part of the beast's once mighty soul.

Travis would pull through – the cleric was tougher than he looked, and that was saying something, comparing him to agile molluskans and walking infernos. Brains compensated for much in Karin, where the local life was crafty, but lacking resourcefulness.

"That's it," Philip jumped, reaching a revelation. "We use their brains against them."

"Care to elaborate, kid?" asked an intrigued Rick.

With his signature smirk, Philip laid out his mapped genius.

"We lead an expedition to the source; full frontal. Take down the savages so fast they can't staunch the water's flow."

"Can't be that easy," doubted Kenneth.

"Kenneth's right. They most likely plan to corrupt the water with a toxin," Hericore said. "I'd know more than anyone the painful feeling of intoxication."

The source's purity was of no concern to Philip. All the Drakeguard needed were flasks of bottled water to travel south; what water remained for Declandale was of no consequence in the pursuit of salvation.

Unfortunately, he knew of Hericore's tethering morality, a special breed of goodness that regarded all life as necessary – a burden to top all burdens.

"We send in Katowa and Lucille. They both have an expert knowledge on chemical warfare," he replied, countering the wave of doubtful thoughts. "Hell, send in Harlan, too. If worst comes to worst, he can vaporise the contamination." Standing proud, Philip watched Hericore's beak let out acceptance.

"This is why I love you, Philip. A problem solver, through and through."

Rick joined in on the praise, leaving Kenneth the only one to not hold him up on a podium.

"Right, let's get this assault team assembled," he smirked, leaving the tent, and Kenneth's sour attitude, behind. Back in the heat and his ego well-stroked, Philip called the Drakeguard in for a roll call."Right lads and ladies, we need a serious talk!" he yelled, beckoning everyone to him.

"Philip, wait a minute," Hericore called, exiting the tent along with Rick.

"Time's wasting, big bird. Best get go–"

"This isn't the best course of action."

It was *that* point in the planning again; the point where Hericore undermined every ounce of progress he sought to make and replaced it with inadequate substitutes.

"What do you mean? I have a solid idea."

"I have a request to make," Rick said.

"Go ahead," Philip allowed.

"You're a natural Greycoat, kid," praised Rick, only without any admiration. "You're a tactician with a mind for combat."

"*I am* pretty great," Philip smiled, basking in the kind words, only to be sucker-punched with the big 'but'.

"Except that's all you have, a mind for combat. I don't think joining the battle would be a wise move," Rick finished.

The Drakeguard now surrounded him, all to witness Rick's negative comment, becoming an audience to a tragedy.

"Ah, come on guys, I can pull my weight. I only clock in at ninety pounds, minimum," he cheerfully said. In a hasty attempt to retrieve his burst bubble, nothing but a deep hole awaited him. Neither Hericore nor Rick wavered their opinions.

"This is a serious thing to ask of you," Hericore said, unmoved. "For your safety."

"Safety, schmafety. I can handle this. Right, Ricky, my man? It's my destiny to help people. 'A hero in the making'. *Ah*? *Ah*?" he said, reminding the detective of his own words.

"I was... hasty in my decision," admitted the turncoat Greycoat. "You're a mastermind, and that's all I saw."

The more he was denied, the more Philip's charm collapsed into a puddle, forming a murky and unworthy tantrum.

"But I helped find the hideout. I formed a plan of attack. Actually… what haven't I helped with?!"

"True. But after speaking with Hericore about your experience – and suffice to say, it's not extensive – we've choose to play your strengths."

"Phil's fought before," defended Helena. "He saved us from–"

"That was luck. Luck and godly favour. A stream of favour that no longer runs for us," Hericore said.

Rick came close, patted him on the shoulder, and sighed. "I overestimated your skills, kid. I'm sorry."

The criticism felt disingenuous. They didn't mean it, they couldn't. They believed in him before today. Again, the paranoid parts of Philip's mind mixed with a rising wave of cranial pain; slowly, a reasonable ploy formed.

Kenneth Porter, a man of questionable past and motives, a man who walked in the wake of both Philip's mentors, had changed their perceptions overnight. A lowly fisherman was capable of manipulating minds of better men, all in an effort to thwart Philip's progress: all to doom the world.

From behind Hericore, emotionless, Kenneth watched his undoing, and hesitant spite grew in his bowels. The Ripper was working his magic – there was no other answer in the kid's aching mind.

"I can survive!" Philip begged, "I weathered Fort Palmer–"

"The way I heard it from Zarp, you stumbled through that mess," Hemora corrected. Even the toadies had taken arms against him. The Ripper's reach was growing.

"Oh, shut it, you overgrown crab; I achieved the unachievable. I travelled time, saw the past *and* the future. More than you or that crusty shell could ever imagine," Philip lashed out.

"You can talk. What's that travesty you're wearing?"

"It's a poncho," Harlan confirmed.

"The fuck's a poncho?"

"A little cloak you wear over your shoulders. Keeps the dust off your clothes," Rangar answered. "Terribly ugly."

They attempted to diffuse tension with a humorous air, but Philip was in no mood for a group paupers' jokes.

"Screw you. Like a fish would know anything about fashion or formality. I'm a better man, a better *hero*, than you'll ever be."

"Yet here you are, running from the law with me, no more a man or hero than I am," Hemora replied in a tone of unfamiliar hatred. Fusing sarcasm and mirth with anger was an irritating thing, growing the molluskan's already deep pools of bubbling arrogance.

"Look, Philip, just sit this one out. There's more to goodness than glory," Hericore said.

"No, it's not fair. It's never fair," Philip whined. "I saved you from Giovanni, I saved all of you lot from Refracted Light, and I'm not just sitting this out!"

Mired in a red face, and spit lying lazily on his chin, he'd become what he never thought he'd be. The prisoners had turned him into a monster for just a few moments, and that was far too long. While a calming breeze accompanied a calming voice from within, the knife was twisted further.

"Can you kill?" Rick asked. "Have you killed?"

"I–"

"He hasn't killed anyone. Dandies never do," Hemora said.

"And you know this from experience?" Holding back nothing, Philip lashed back with more than just words. Stepping in close, he grabbed the fish's slimy neck; breathing was allowed, but talking was not. "I've read your file, I know what you are. You've hung around with many dandies in the past. A flamboyant bunch, for sure. Oh, and something far worse is scribbled in those pages too... Shall I tell them, Vangesh?"

"You dare."

"Philip, this has to end," snapped Hericore, but he was too far gone.

Daringly, Philip annoyingly half-smiled and claimed, "better to be called 'dandy' than 'nonce', aye, Vangesh?"

Pushed away and grappled, Hemora's violent reply said it all. Panting in fearful rage, the fish had one too many skeletons in his closet. He was losing the argument, but won the moral high ground.

"I'll kill you! You lying bast-" Rangar stepped in to wrestle them apart, dragging away Hemora while the screams continued, "-you son of a – SCREW YOU! I'll kill you, you wimpy pot of lies!"

With the whole group ganging up on him, Philip saw only two options: to let it go or to prove he *could* kill, using Hemora as an ample subject. Luckily for the molluskan, he chose the former. And perhaps it was the right choice; he'd never know. Rick seemed to think so, and gave one last nugget of advice.

"All leaders must pull back at some point. Make this your first, kid."

"Fine! Time to sit out." With that, Philip stormed back into the tent, closing it off from the outside world. Helena offered her comfort, but he declined, as he did with Hericore's sympathy and Kenneth's lying words.

He was denied his true potential before, and that didn't end well. He lost a love as she befell a disgusting end. Never again. As he remembered her, his mind turned to ending it all, to be with her again. Etheriam held promise, but being under the thumb of the gods was not an appealing concept.

As he'd done before, Philip rejected death in hopes of besting the twisted state of being entirely. If he wouldn't succumb to death, then death would bow to him.

Now, Hericore sought to stifle his promise, wanting to neuter all his fighting spirit and transform him into nothing but a suited commander, cowering behind the guise of safety; using the wrappings of moral goodness like chains to bind the warring side in Philip.

Then anger turned to Kenneth, the mystery man, the only variable unaccounted for, never present in any of his predictive dreams, cloaked in purple mist; the outlier in a sea of knowledge. If anyone could whisper into Hericore's ear and persuade the drake of Philip's transformation, it was Kenneth and a shroud of uncertainty.

Scared of where his true allies remained, Philip watched through the tent's flap as Rick led Lucille, Haruka, and Harlan, with the jester Hemora, too. For once, he wished the plan to fail and purge the group of that idiot fish for good.

Paradise never felt so far from his reach, and with the visions gone, fear had control again. It would take a miracle to rescue his soul from the creeping dark of fear, and a miracle was exactly what Philip received. A motivator so strong, it snapped a semblance of sense into him.

***

Philip lost his rage and found a pleasant sleep in the comfort of the tent: a place free from the Guards' brash comments. This sleep held more insight for him, and premiered the future; this time was foggy though, and appeared through murky eyes and black smoke.

He was standing atop a tower above all else, looking out on a grey ocean as it swallowed the landscape in gnawing bites. Lightning struck the ocean to no avail, making no sound, carrying no current. The skies above were black, as were the finer details of the tower.

A purgatory of feeling, he felt no rage, sorrow, joy; only a speck of mortality grasped him. This was until an inky figure climbed the tower to oppose him. It was Kenneth, without a murmur of the fisherman he knew. Holding his illethium pride in one hand and a fist of steel in the other, Kenneth was a vengeful spectre that charged forward with extreme prejudice.

Philip jolted awake, after feeling the cold, sharp pain of the sword meeting his chest. Though only a dream, the blade's edge haunted him in the waking world. Seeing this vision of what was coming left a deep sense of hopelessness in him. Kenneth was to slay him? Never had a dream shown a falsity, but this couldn't be; he couldn't die.

An hour passed and his pondering mind was wrapped in fearful thoughts of the future. Many people faced life with confidence knowing death wouldn't snatch them today. But one day, Philip would stand above all else knowing that day was his last, and Kenneth would be the one to do it.

Denial followed, claiming that he woke before the sword made contact, and that it might not be over. The denial festered and evolved into a new hope as his nerves slowly soothed at the healing smells from Travis' herbal medicine. Seeing the stump where Travis' leg once was made him think of the fractured Vagabonds and why they fell apart. Soon he'd be gone, and the 'Bonds would thin out even more.

"I refuse to die, I can't," Philip muttered. The phase was said again and again, until a friendly face decided to come back from the brink. "This whole damn journey I've been holding the short end of the stick."

Travis' mouth stretched open and said, "You mean 'wrong end of the stick' boyo."

Chapter 10: Rose's Rule

Ash and the Cult fled far and fled fast. What happened at the Fork was reckless terrorism, and that was the worst kind of terror: without a point.

While the Order was busy killing each other, the four continued to run, and put at least a couple of miles between them and the trade post before finally stopping to collect their shambled wits.

The sun was waking by the time they'd halted in what seemed to be a recent holdover near Lake Vita, cramped under a deserted bridge. Ravaged patches of mushrooms surrounded a pit of embers in a camp for the downtrodden; a fitting place for the Cult.

"Can't I go one night without being bloody attacked?" Ash said.

"No one's that lucky these days," Dallas answered, as she and Natalia started to unpack their dwindling amount of equipment.

Roy's Fork was supposed to be a place of rest and recuperation, but that honour now rested on this empty land. They clamoured for the chance to use what remained of the squandered day; all weak, all weary.

"The Beast will keep watch till nine, then I'll take over," Natalia ordered, unrolling her bedding and cautiously reaching sleep.

"Are we not going to discuss the crazed man that shot at us?" Donsis asked.

"Not much to talk about," Dallas shrugged. "And he wasn't after us. He was aiming for the Order's fodder. Wouldn't be remiss to believe that crazed 'man' to be a crazed undead like us. The Order picks their enemies by the bunch."

The shooter was too far from view, but the target was all too close to both him and the Drakeguard.

"He shot down a face familiar to me."

"That bald kid?" Dallas asked.

"Yep, called Hunter, he was. Earned the name, too. Met him a year back, a captive of Fort Palmer. A rare talent with a golden heart."

Hunter was young now, but seemed even more so back then – a youthful lad. Along with several other rejects of society, the lad built his talents under the supervision of the vampires ruling Palmer, all until the Order arrived, and he quickly turned traitor.

The only Palmer survivor who hadn't travelled the passage of time, Hunter failed to witness the Prophecy of Chyenne, and was stuck on a sharp fence between the Order and Hericore.

The prophecy was the Drakeguard's only compass: showing the way forward, but only one direction. The worlds told of the old king of gold, and that was all Hericore needed to start their escapades south. One line of one prophecy, a single, thousand year-old line, changed the lives of so many.

Ash just wanted it to be a line of truth. Many good men did bad things because of poorly-worded messages from the gods. Vagueness spelled the end for so many people of equal ignorance; he wouldn't join them.

"The brat didn't seem so skilled," Dallas said.

"Whoever attacked him wasn't your run-of-the-mill killer. He was more," Donsis replied.

"Meet many killers in your day, Donsis?" Ash said, sceptical of the elf's knowledge regarding violence.

"I can't fight a wounded mouse. Hired help is all I know."

He'd seen Donsis parade the streets of Valordolt before, wrapped in a regiment containing old dogs of war, a cheap army of cripples and greyed folks that weathered the Wastern Wars. Buying wounded warriors was cheap, but back then, damn near everything was cheap.

Ash's wife's dowry had been a sum of six casts and a cleaver capable of rending the world. A small reward for tackling marriage – especially for a spinster – but it wasn't the dowry he married for, it was love. Ironically, the dowry was all that remained now.

"Glad we have Beast to watch our asses. I'd hate to run into any more 'hired help'," Dallas said.

"You think he wasn't hired?" Donsis said, with concern.

"Aye, that was the work of a freelancer."

"Ohh, she's good. Not good on the eyes... But good," crept a flamboyant voice from the distance, echoing around the woodlands. Ash recoiled and grabbed his axe – if they'd been followed, then the fight wasn't over.

"What's wrong?" Dallas questioned, tilting her head. Given her look, it was apparent that the calling was meant for him, and him alone.

Many things could project their cries, some not even human – more of the grotesque, beastly sort.

"Didn't you hear that?" Donsis asked her.

"Nope, they didn't. Only you lucky two," said the voice once more, this time louder and eerier than the first. Was this an illusionist, hoping to rob them blind with his ethereal art? Maybe a formless one, made of the very shadows in the air?

"Show yourself!" Ash valiantly shouted.

"With pleasure," said the voice.

A feeling of exhaust forced all the air from his lung, and energy burnt in his muscles, leaving them heavy.

"Ash, tone it down. I need rest," complained Natalia.

"He's not right, Nat. Give him some Opi," suggested Dallas in a panicked motion made all too late.

A soft, child's lullaby filled the forest, exclusively for the Adonis duo. Pitched perfectly, it was as if a choir of children were present, chanting out the lyrics to this lulling tune. The children sung well, but did so in distress; the unsettling vibes of horror stabbed at the mind, reducing Ash to a slobbering state.

"This song…" the dwarf mumbled, wading into fuzzy thoughts, "it's..."

"It's Rose's Rule. My mother would play this on a music box. She'd sing to me, and I'd mimic it with a timid hum," Donsis slurred.

"Correct!" cheered the voice. "This song accompanied my downfall. It's only fitting that it introduce yours."

From that point onward – Ash's vision and hearing began to slowly recede, and he fell to the ground in a gentle manner.

Compared to his mental fights with Donsis, this felt like total domination, with every part of his head numb, and the voice becoming louder and louder, eventually breaking into an elongated laugh.

***

When the laughter was no longer a torment, Ash's eyes opened. Dallas and Natalia didn't await him – there was only a thick black fog stretching into an endless abyss. Spanning infinitely in all directions, the black landscape was his heaven above and hell below; an endless sea of cursed nothing.

From the distance came a sob. It was pitched high, with waves of deep, warped wails too. This was a memory; one that should've stayed buried. Never wanting to approach the husk, Ash stood firm. But it seemed if he wasn't going to face it, it would face him.

Slow at first, the horrid mess came to view. A slender dwarf, draped in white linen with black, flowing hair came to view. She crawled on all fours, with a face as blue as the sky, and eyes green as the grass. Her rasping breath was loud and unnerving, and she shimmered in the misted realm; never here nor there.

"No," Ash whimpered. This wasn't happening, it couldn't. In an instant, all pretence of bravery and heroism was lost, and he adopted Donsis' fear, four-fold.

The creature picked up speed, sprinting like a limber beast on all fours. Making the remaining distance in seconds, she popped up before him and screamed. This deafening scream was one of pain.

"Why?! Why, why, why?!"

"I don't know. Please, I–"

Going white in the face, Ash soon lost the ability to think and stand. Passing out again, he heard a low chuckle, familiar to the one he'd heard before.

Coming back to his senses, eventually, he was free from the ghostly regret.

"What's this mess? Answer me, foul demon," he bellowed in an exhausted voice.

"This my dear, Ashley, is no mess at all. Rather, it's the confines of your own sub-conscious." The same voice called out to him, from everywhere and nowhere, holding equal panache. Whoever owned this voice was special – a childish feeling came from it, but also an underlying sense of danger, breaching every ounce of privacy he had.

"My what?"

"Your *mind!*" the voice spelled out.

Streaks of lightning blasted in the distance, connecting into a dull network of occasional brilliance, as several strikes chained together, forming a wondrous display.

"Always knew I was empty up there," Ash acknowledged. "Nothing but sawdust."

"Yes, quite. Still better than some of your friends, no? That Beast's head is all hissing and barking; it's like peering into a rabies-filled zoo. I prefer your vacuous thinker by a country mile. 'Twas once empty, but no longer," said the voice, "For *I* have come for a rather spontaneous visit."

"I don't take to kindly to visitors. So please, fuck –off."

"Ha! Never the gentlemen. No matter. I've brought a gift to warm this tundra of a mind."

The voice's breathing grew and ceased to surround Ash's every angle, eventually forming into a single body. It was a slender man, who stood tall and proud. His face was obscured by a white porcelain mask, shaped tightly around the flesh, with the only facial features visible being a Cheshire smile and two shiny, clover green eyes, teeming with glee and ill intent.

He wore the outfit of a classic court jester, bells and all, with the chequered pattern on his chest resembling a deck of cards, all black and red. Above the jester's attire was a wreath of clovers around his neck, and an unusually tall top hat capping off the erratic outfit.

The mask was by far the worst part; being responsible for all of Ash's unease. The smile was large – inhuman – lined with a thick and glossy lipstick, coloured a familiar green. Though white, the mask was old, and discolouration was in full effect.

The slender one's approach was joined by the bitter taste of stout, and the taste planted itself in Ash's mouth without permission, an ongoing theme with this being; first Ester Valley, now this.

He grew more disgruntled with this clown, and reached for the axe upon his back, lustful with the idea of cleaving down this trickster – but it was to no avail; the weapon was gone.

"Tut, tut. There's no conventional weapons in here, Ashley. Especially when *I* come to play," the jester mocked. It was rare that a threat walked Magnus and couldn't be crushed. Ash bit the bullet and surrendered to a more learned approach.

"Then if my muscles won't stop you, then perhaps my words can?"

"If these words aren't 'fuck', 'off', or a combination of the two, then go ahead..."

"Is it really you? Or are you just a blurred illusion like at Ester?"

A streak of fear rose in this question, fear that he didn't want to admit to. It was fear unfettered, not a taint from Donsis, but true, untapped fear.

"Can't I be both? Ha, indeed, it is I. I suppose I should roll out the welcome wagon... *I* am the Trapmaster, Meddler of Minds and Finder of Thoughts. The legend is real, and my hand is unjust," said the Master, bored with such a typical introduction. "And since Roy's Fork, I've been stalking you, Ashley Belwert. You and your little crew of broken fighters are rather *interesting*, just like your old crew."

"There've been countless tales about you, and I'd be a fool to doubt them now. You've tangled with my friends, and now I ask – why me? Why come back for me?"

Another pause; the Trapmaster loved suspense and theatrics more than logic.

"You've got something I want."

Things of legend sought things of equal fame. Ash had no doubts that the Trapmaster sought the Time Stone, and it was something he couldn't help with, even if he shared such a bad idea. The Stone was most likely dead, along with his friends at Ester Valley.

"I have nothing to give. You caught me at a bad time, mate. Death leaves little reward."

"Haha-hoo! Very funny," replied the Trapmaster, with a natural, sarcastic voice. "No. What I require is not physical, but rather something you know."

"Again, caught me at a bad time. My head may be huge, but my brain isn't. I'm the definition of a dumb-ass," he replied, keeping his mind and lips sealed from this mental thief.

"Tut tut, all too coy, my dear boy. Ashley, Ashley, Ashley–"

"Don't...! Don't call me that."

"But that is your name, is it not?" Ash remained silent. The masterful trapper wanted only one thing: weakness. Feeding off man's weaker parts, the Master found little nourishment in his steadfast personality. "Oh Ashley, I'm going to have fun breaking you in."

Another lullaby took him into an even darker place, which eventually dissipated to reveal a new location. A chunk of the past was ripped from his head and replicated before them. They stood amidst the battle in Ester Valley, the place where he died in order for Adonis to live.

It was frozen in place, and every screaming paladin was remembered in immaculate detail. The blood-drunk Wildcats, and even Opyus, had presence in the scene set for his displeasure. The heat of combat was missing, replaced with a chilling void of the senses; no smell, sound, or feeling made for an uncanny recollection.

Guilt was a tumour at times: building slowly within. This recreation was nothing but an accelerant, forcing guilt to grow in Ash, bursting the heart, forcing tears on the periphery of his vision. He hadn't felt this bad in years, if ever; the Trapmaster was in his head, in more ways than one.

"Please. No," he begged, as a storm of traumatic stress took hold, a clenching tightness that drained his will.

"Nice to see the old place," the Trapmaster said, "but ever so lonely. I think you need a friend."

With a whistle, a great weight plucked from within his head and gut, pulling away his fears and panic. A second body formed beside the Master, and this one was a recognisable face. "May I present this most honoured guest," the Trapmaster grandly introduced. "Greed incarnate, the Killer of Loan Sharks, and Swimmer of Sewers... Donsis Allisteel!"

Chapter 11: Black and White Truths

Donsis felt real for the first time since Valordolt; physically, at least. On the inside, he felt hollow and a husk of what was once a proud elf. His sense of self wavered as he stood beside the Trapmaster. The man was the stuff of legend back home, and his fear raced against excitement to meet the real deal.

Schools of scholars feared the reaper of thoughts, and dismissed the stories as propaganda. But every kid remembered two myths when they become men: the Bogeyman, and the Trapmaster. One was already proven real, and now the second stood beside him. However, this legend was in no mood to talk trivialities, as he soon found out.

The Master passed him by in silence, and a pungent smell of raspberries radiated from the mythical man, filling him with joy. Ash joined his side, and they watched the jester spin around the area in a dancing manoeuvre, examining each gory picture painted in the memory.

Donsis hadn't witnessed true war, only feeling the after-shocks tremor through the world. The tragedy scattered around them was above the worst rung of his imagination. It was the crying teen, torn limb from limb that got to him; he never could stomach the suffering of children.

"Beautiful, isn't it?" asked the Trapmaster. Donsis failed to answer, moved by this sick sight, recently conjured. "Don't answer, then. I know you're impressed. All this *life*, all these *minds*: the chaos... All ended *so* easily."

"Good to see you in one piece again," Ash said to him. The dweller looked sad, slowly being weakened to something less than a man. Maybe this was why he presented friendship? "How's my brain been treating you?"

"Fair. But boringly barren." It was a jape that hit softly, meant to lighten the heart. Ash returned a smile, one that warmed the chilled setting, but only just. Looking up, the moon on high was replaced with the Master's own cheeky grin, even the stars held conniptions geared toward the coming carnage. Donsis felt it, and Ash spoke it.

"Think we'll survive this? Trapmaster's not known for his mercy; it's the ground or the loony bin, right?"

"Obviously not. He needs us. I've been on the receiving end of 'useless', and trust me, we'd be disposed of by now. Warden Hart, he is not."

In the mind, memories were the only treasure worth plundering. Donsis had been locked in Ash's head for a couple of days now, and could never find out where the memories were locked away. He doubted the Trapmaster would have more luck. Some treasures should stay hidden, forever.

"You're selling my abilities a wee bit short, Donsis. Don't bother answering; I know you're doubting me. I can *sense it!*" the Trapmaster yelled in a shrill chord, as he backed away and took a seat on what seemed to be a non-existent chair. With a tip of the hat, he giggled like a child. "I'm quite good."

"What is it you want? What do I know?" Ash questioned.

"Well, I know that you know about a certain Tempus Porta. The Time Stone, Ashley. I want your memories, all of the ones pertaining to it, and those that have it now."

What a madman could want with a Primal Stone was depressing thought. Donsis tried not to dwell on it; never being fond of the act, or the practitioners of it.

The Trapmaster, being a self-made man of supposed benevolence, summoned a chess table from thin air. "Since I'm a nice little joker, I'll even gamble for it. *One* game of chess, winner takes the memories," he offered, as the metallic pawns and knights rose out of the board, sitting in wait.

"No deal. I already own the memories," Ash claimed. "I gain nothing from agreeing."

Sounding sour, the Master stroked a non-existent beard and snapped his fingers. "What about this, Ashley?"

A green gem, similar to an opal, hovered over the table. Ash snapped at it, clawing at it to no effect, his hands cutting through it like smoke.

"Sweet enough for ya? This is Mentir Mania, or the 'Mind Stone' as you'd call it. If *you* win, this is your prize."

Donsis knew this was a trick. If the Trapmaster was a mind reader, then playing a game of strategy built upon sharpening the mind was a stupid move. Even when dangling the Mind Stone before them, they had to decline.

Before he could discuss this with Ash, the hot-headed dwarf had answered. "Game on!" He took a seat on the opposing side of the board and engaged the Trapmaster in a battle for his very memories.

Surrounded by the long lost and those who had made them so, the location of this match was demoralising enough to wrangle an early submission from any normal man. But then, neither he nor Ash were part of 'mankind', the spawn of fearful jealousy.

Donsis planted himself between the two, overlooking both sides of the board from a different perspective. The hopes of an epiphany were slim, but existent.

"I'll warn you of this much," the Trapmaster gloated. "I've spent many a year winning at chess."

"A chess master, a mind master, yet still you can't just take my memories?" Ash replied.

"I'd love nothing more than your memories on Hericore's little escapade, juicy and ripe for the taking. But the devil's in the details."

"What do you mean. What details?"

"When your minds interlocked into one seductive little minx, the surgery bound the memory cellulose shut. A mentally locked door, if you will. As the owners, you have full access to this door, while I'm left out in the cold streets of the abyss."

"We're stuck here thanks to you and you can't leave because of us?" Ash realised.

"A stalemate, then," Donsis added, with his suspicions going wild.

Even now, he could tell of a trick in hiding – a lack of such a thing would be ill-fitting of the Trapmaster's title.

"Ash, reconsider this," Donsis said, but the advice struggled to reach past dwarven bravado.

"Relax, else you'll put me off."

"White moves first," said the Trapmaster, as he spun the board around, forcing Ash to play as the white army, initiating the game.

While Ash planned an offensive, Donsis spent time understanding his predicament, but still couldn't figure it all out. If he was unconscious in the waking world, then shouldn't Dallas or Natalia see the Trapmaster and his enthralling spells?

These thoughts did not need any expression, and the Trapmaster still heard them – words became unnecessary with this psychic. "Think, Donsis! I am, as I claimed, 'quite good'. Filtering the perceptions of those undead rejects is simplicity itself," the Trapmaster said, interrupting his thoughts.

"I've dined with illusionists before. Never has the act of sifting perception arisen," Donsis said inquisitively.

"Those whose money you've grown bloated with, all of them are cheap reflections of my own art. Ethereal magic is a mere child of the child of my own power. Filtering perceptions can make even the most observant soul turn a blind eye. A gift that serves me well – as escape and I go hand in hand."

Donsis didn't like the feeling of his mind being invaded, abused and bent. It was akin to being mocked by a ghost with no way to silence him, all he can do was let him tire.

Ash finally touched a piece, and on contact, it morphed into a figure close to both their pasts. Soon, all the pieces, white and black, twisted into graven images.

"Did either of you know that in the beginnings of chess, both sides of the board had a unique look to them?" asked the Trapmaster.

"Can't say I did," they answered in unison.

"Typical; the mark of a dullard is fleeting facts," tutted the Trapmaster, before finishing his little trivia. "Originally, the whites were soldiers of the Order, and the blacks took shape of a demonic horde – minotaurs and the like. But over the years things changed, the Order darkened themselves, tarnishing their image, and soon the game reflected this; now black and white are all soldiers of vitality, old and new."

With a face of shame, Ash weakly stated, "I'm no demon."

Looking down at the board, the faces newly carved into the chess pieces were those of the Drakeguard, crafted with fine detail.

The king resembled Hericore's long, scaly head, the faithful queen was Zarpadon, and the bishops had Travis' wild mop of hair. The knights showed Philip riding Thomas, an ever loyal steed, and the rooks sat to the sides, lonesome with Helena's beauty. As for the pawns, they all had the face of Ash wielding his beloved axe, a chilling site to witness.

The Trapmaster was burrowing under Ash's skin in all the right ways. The dwarf's look was that of distraction – not the ideal look for a chess player of little experience.

"You're quite dashing in figurine form. Now play on, if it please you."

"Why chess?" asked Donsis.

"I believe in fairness. I usually test my associates with a riddle or puzzle. But today, I feel like a good game of chess," the Trapmaster replied. "Come on, Ashley, we haven't got all night. Oh, wait… we do."

Ash made a snap decision, and moved the farthest right pawn forward two spaces; a bold but careless strategy.

"Maybe I should play in your place," Donsis suggested, but the request was denied.

"It's not your foul memories I long for."

The trapper's weakness seemed unclear throughout the countless tales, and that never boded well. Ash, on the other hand, possessed many weaknesses. Rage, heroism, dim wit: all of these were bad enough. Yet more weaknesses kept flowing from the dwarf, courtesy of the Trapmaster.

"I never visited my cousin after I dreamt of kissing her soft, cherry lips," said the pawn, in a high pitched replica of Ash's own voice.

"I should mention the little twist I added to this dull game: every move you make comes at a cost. That cost is a secret. Move the pawns and you, Donsis will bear witness to some of Ashley's worst moments. As you lose more and more, the secrets run deeper and deeper, until you lose the game... or your dignity," said the Trapmaster, with a devilish smile cutting up into his cheeks at an almost inhuman level.

"And if I don't move a pawn?" Ash hesitated to ask.

"That would be telling."

Determined not to be dissuaded, Ash watched his opponent's move, and planned accordingly. The next piece to move was a knight, and with it, a message straight from Philip's mouth.

"Gods give me strength with that dwarven guy. His melon's missing some seeds, if you ask me."

"Ah, so if I move a royal piece, *that* happens," Ash said, discomforted by the dismissive words.

"A treat I plucked from the heads of your so called 'friends' the last time we met," explained the Trapmaster. "These are their *real* opinions of Ashley Belwert."

Ashley was the name used by the Master, and this sired confusion within Donsis. Was it a pet name, or a secret yet to pour from a pawn's mouth?

"You've met the Drakeguard before?" the elf asked, allowing Ash time to fortify his focus.

"Yes. We met back in the belly of the beast, the same day that Ashley was saved. Philip, Helena, Zarpadon, Travis and the two meat-heads, James and Thomas, if memory serves me... Which it always does, *mind* you." Chuckling again, the Trapmaster set a rook on the rampage, claiming a pawn. "Philip had quite the mouth on him. He better not have what I'm looking for."

"What *are* you looking for? It's obvious you know where the Time Stone is. So don't patronise me, and tell the truth."

"Do you ever tell the truth? 'Course not, it's not fun otherwise," said the Trapmaster angrily, having finally lost a piece to Ash. "I will reveal all in good time. That is, if you make it that far."

The end of life, *his* life, had scared Donsis before now, but looking around at the battle that Ash perished in was a truly fearful event. He died betrayed in an office, cold and unsupported, but now he had a second chance, a chance he wasn't ready to squander.

Fortune favoured the brave, and he was never a brave man – it was then logical that favour was against the aged elf. And when the Trapmaster offered Ash a deal with the devil – one that could end the power struggle of Adonis in its prime – how could he have expected anything else?

Chapter 12: Mastering Traps

Ash never believed in fairy-tales – he scoffed at stories containing such whimsy. But now, face to face with a real monster of bed-time terror, he felt the fool for never believing.

When the chess pieces sung his secrets to Donsis, a sense of vulnerability dug deep in his body and mind, allowing the Trapmaster to, in turn, dive into those crevasses and exploit him further.

Vulnerability tended to breed rapidly, and in time, nothing but weakness was left to inhabit a shell of one's former self.

Ashley was his name. This unkind truth spilled next, and it was more humiliating than scarring. Yet every secret that wasn't his worst wasn't his defeat, giving him respite. If his biggest regrets were ever shown, it'd be his darkest day – a day where he'd have to face the cracked reality behind him.

"Using your queen this early can be... irresponsible, Ashley," said the Trapmaster, then mimicking his move. "I think I'll do the same."

Holding strong, he replied, "You can't strike yellow in me."

"It seems already have." With another giggle, the Trapmaster raised a finger and flicked the colour of marigolds into Ash's skin. The change lasted only a few seconds, but the terror lingered in the dwarf far long.

As the match went on, Donsis walked circles around them, as if a new angle would give away either of their strategies. After more pawns fell, Donsis found his secrets amusing, snickering under guilty breaths at them. This didn't make things easier.

The game seemed to be lost after a host of bad decisions; the Trapmaster had only lost what he needed in order to seem beatable. Meanwhile, Ash had six pieces left, and they were dropping faster than actual soldiers during war.

"Come on, you can recover. Just keep Travis close to Hericore, and you should be fine," Donsis said reassuringly, but he heard the doubt hidden deep within the motivation.

Another pawn left the fight – just one measly infantryman remained and was forced to brave the king alone. The Trapmaster's annoying amount of happiness was growing palpable; that was, until he finally made a mistake. Ash used his last knight to lock the Master's king in check.

"What? How?!" snarled the Trapmaster, as his smarmy attitude turned to ashes in an instant. "Now, Ashley, please. Let me retract that last move. I'll make it worth your while."

Ash became overwhelmed with intrigue. What kind of deal would a mind invader have to offer? The beggar rarely had leverage over a lord.

"What deal do you have in mind?"

"Let me retry that move and save my precious queen. In return, I'll remove Donsis from your head. I'll rip him out into the nothingness and let him fade away," offered the Trapmaster; and what an offer it was.

Donsis yelped and immediately argued against it.

"Don't do this. He's playing you for a fool. Don't back down now."

The deal was a juicy offering, but either choice was problematic – trust the powerless friend or the powerful enemy? Both options left him at a disadvantage and powerless in his own right, something he always despised.

The Trapmaster fabricated two documents before Ash, asking him to sign off his choice.

"It doesn't get simpler than this. Pick quickly, Ashley," the Master grinned, handing a blood-soaked quill to place his signature.

"Please," begged Donsis, bent down on his knobbly knees. "You'd be literally signing my life away. I was sentenced to death twice before. Not again."

The strain of indecision rocked Ash's morals to the core, and nothing happened for a solid minute, as he slowly grabbed the quill and pouted.

"This is the decision you've always longed for," claimed the Trapmaster. "The Hero's Calling."

The call of heroism grabbed him, but never had Ash had to make that all-important choice: suffering of the self to prevent another's atrocity. Little more consideration needed to be made – Donsis was a vile rat, a bigoted piece of vermin. But this didn't give him the right to end the elf's life.

"No deal. We keep playing, and I'm going to win."

Donsis jumped into the air and cheered, but the Trapmaster just kept smiling.

"Shame. I honestly thought you'd give in to me. Your loss, really," he said, planting a pawn on Ash's end of the board, transcending into a queen and putting Hericore in check. "It seems you've fallen for my trap. Heh!"

"Oh, darn," exclaimed a somewhat defeated Donsis, as the struggle persisted. As expected, Ash didn't have a choice – he never did, never had; he was a pawn in his own right.

"Your move," said the Trapmaster, gazing politely at the duo, anticipating their downfall.

With his last, hopeless move, Ash placed his pawn at the feet of the enemy king, and practically surrendered.

"My wife was sick. Medicine couldn't help her pains. Only a pillow would suffice," said the pawn, as the last secret poured from its mouth.

Donsis didn't laugh this time – how could he? What happened to the sweet-hearted spinster couldn't be forgotten, and the Trapmaster just highlighted how futile it was to bury the past.

Placing a palm of platitude on his shoulder, the elf consoled him, wholeheartedly. The Master had won; the white king still remained, but with no soldiers, it was over.

"Well done, well done," clapped the Trapmaster. "A bold response, saving Donsis; perhaps even the right choice. But why bother to save the scum?"

It was another question that demanded little pause. "I saved a life today. That was the right choice. I, Ashley Belwert, did 'quite good'."

With a stance of pride, he stared down the Trapmaster, managing to awake a dormant dragon, breathing shallow breaths in the face of the Master's own broken persona.

Screaming in a voice unlike his own, much lighter and fearful, the Trapmaster blasted hate at Ash's minor, personal victory.

"Quite good? That's a rich statement from you." the Trapmaster continued, dropping bolts of wrathful lighting down onto the recreation of Ester Valley. "At your very core, a disgusting man looms, one that has done disgusting things! At Palmer, you slaughtered many recluse and scholarly vampires without an inkling of remorse – I'd know. The very nerve to seek a paragon's path is hypocrisy at its finest, you cur."

Though it was the ramblings of an insane man, Ash saw the reasoning behind it.

"Yes, I am a monstrous cur. That is way I seek to redeem myself. I need to honour the dead, not the living," Ash admitted, in a spur of honesty. "My friends, yours, even the Order, all their deaths can't be for nought. I can't take lives in vain again."

In the swirling madness, the Trapmaster finally showed a true emotion towards him; sympathy.

"You really want to save this horrid world? Even with all the wrong?"

"Always."

"Then I'm sorry, that wasn't me talking. Old habits." Coughing back his original tone, the Master slumped back in his seat and took a sad breath.

"If I could turn back time, I would," Ash consoled.

"You can," reminded Donsis.

"More important things lie on the path ahead. I'd be foolish to waste the Time Stone in this harsh, eleventh hour." It was at that moment, that Ash looked inward, at his own foolish thinking. "The boys have a job to do. The ones in Karin are the real heroes. I can chase them all damn day, but I'm just patchwork now."

"I see that now," the Trapmaster said with a sense of condolence. "I may have misjudged you, Ashley."

"The fault is mine," Ash replied, with solace, holding a humble vibration close to his heart.

With a thunderous clap from the Master's hand, the scene of carnage disappeared, evaporating like steam. Soon, only the dark, stormy void remained.

"Well, I found what I was looking for. Goodbye, Adonis. May your friends down south offer me more of this... revelation."

"Wait. You're just leaving? What of the Mind Stone?" Donsis asked, filling with hope that it'd be offered as some consolation prize.

"I can't let you hurt them. Hericore's like family to me. Patchwork or no, I owe him," Ash warned, asking for more trouble.

"Frankly, you can't stop me," said the Trapmaster, as he vanished in a dash of green light. "Oh, and keep an eye on this 'new family' of yours, Ash. Your old one might get jealous."

Their hearing dulled again, and the mindscape collapsed along with the disappearance of the Mind Stone. Donsis was consumed in a grey mist which was disrupted by a blast of white, and he was blinded with a bright light.

"Thank you," whispered a youthful voice in Ash's ear. It was one of recent memory, but with no face to match.

The light faded and turned to darkness. This persisted until Natalia's worried voice was heard calling to him.

"Wake up, Ash. For the love of Lilith, wake up!"

So he did.

***

Adonis returned to Magnus' soft earth, surrounded by his fellow strange folk. Dallas was whittling something out of the fallen flora, Natalia was examining her books for a solution to his slumber, and the Beast hunched over in isolation.

"Thank Lilith you're alright," praised Natalia, throwing herself into his arms. "You passed out again and wouldn't awake. I thought Donsis had done something stupid." She relaxed, bookmarking the page of her necrotic manifest – just in case.

"See, told you he'd be fine. Just something we undead go through," Dallas said casually.

"No, it was more than that. You were standing straight, face planted downward, relentlessly shaking. It didn't happen like that before, it never has," Natalia refuted.

Ash didn't answer immediately, too pleased by the Trapmaster's mercy, allowing him to walk away unbent.

"I made it," he said, quietly.

"Made it through what..?"

"That was none of Donsis' doing. In fact, I can't even hear him anymore," he replied, desperately trying to locate the whiny voice in his head, but failing.

"So what happened? Had one too many back at the Fork?" asked Dallas.

"No, no, worse than a drunken stupor. I had an audience with *the* Trapmaster." As he told the two, they didn't look convinced. Both looked around to see nothing but the dimmed sun.

"A mythical being from centuries past came and spoke to *you*? You did have too much to drink then," Dallas dismissed, before redirecting her attention back to the figurine she crafted lovingly.

"I'm speaking the truth. He stole my memories. A thing that belonged to *me!*" Ash felt the tingling of Donsis' presence returning, and with it came the feeling of crammed space, coupled with a constant battle for a voice.

"Technically, he won the knowledge. Fair and square-ish," Donsis broke out.

Finding a lost roth was gratifying, but recovering Donsis was finding a larger wealth, one paid in company. Never admitting his joy, Ash kept a plain face while gleaming inside, a feeling shared by his companion.

"Good to see you back," he said.

"Thanks to you," Donsis replied, gratefully. "You're not too bad for a dwellerrr… dwarf."

Earning a change of heart from a heartless man was all the thanks Ash could need. It was nice to see a walking deterrent coming round to society's way of thinking.

"If you both saw him, then it must be true," Natalia said, with wonderment.

"We should be on watch, in case he comes back for more," Donsis suggested.

"Go right ahead. Beast looks tired enough," Dallas said, adding the finishing touches to the wooden figurine and placing it by the fire. "Perfect."

Upon closer examination, he noticed the figure had a striking resemblance to Philip: the waistcoat, pocket watch, and mass of hair all made an uncanny match.

"Dallas, why did you make that particular figurine? Just curious," he asked, hiding all urgency.

"I don't know. I was waiting for you to wake up when it just popped into my head. I do love pretty boys; so dashing."

Ash didn't understand, but after Donsis gave him a push in the right direction, worry dawned on him. The Trapmaster was leaving them a breadcrumb in this world of loss and the lost.

"We need to leave for Karin," he demanded.

"Why, I'm in no rush. Nor can Lilith's work be moved so fast," Natalia replied.

"It's not about your work. It's my friends – they're rowing in creeks of danger."

If the Trapmaster was en-route to the desert in search of Philip and the rest, then the worst was still to come. Ash had taken the first steps to redemption, but with more lives in danger, the work wasn't done, the dream couldn't end, and the paragon's path had to wait.

"Fine. If it please you…" Natalia said, with surprising enthusiasm.

"Right, then. You willing, Donsis?" he rallied.

"I am now. Two heads, right?"

Chapter 13: The Stranger

Harlan was reluctant to join Rick's assault. The way Philip was cast off and mocked was unsettling to witness. But, Lucille's coercion successfully pulled him aboard, and he rode upon Gerald's back with Rick, mitigating the horse's purpose to that of a recovery wagon.

His place on the high horse made watching over Lucille an easy task, one he was thankful for. Haruka's earlier pep talk was great, and both girls' presence now increased the merriment of the mission tenfold.

The girls scouted ahead, marking off the shallow caves around the scorched eastern area; no sign of the source. This stretch of land was known as, the Dunes, and curled around Declandale like a crescent moon, dipping a hundred miles south, all the way to Slab City. The Dunes were desolate, uninhabitable to most, but the bandits they sought lingered somewhere – the cockroaches forged a burrow.

After burning out Philip's ego faster than the Karinese sun, Hemora marched to the side of his horse, chatting away with Rick. Their words were boring, fantasising over weaponry and politics, both lesser subjects in Harlan's mind. A century spent on each subject, little time remained in his lengthy life for either.

As they led a crusade around the dry plains, the warm sun never bothered to itch the surface of his brown skin – a thankful reason to be Karinese.

The bannasite burns were a whole other matter. He found it so ironic that a man of his fetish could be so pained by burning, and was embarrassed to admit this discomfort.

Heat never fazed him, but the effects of dehydration did, and whether a mirage or distant illusion, blurred figures danced on the horizon, calling to him in forgotten speech. The deserts held many ghosts that could very well be roaming around under the orange blaze, but this was unlikely. Spirits only were attracted to the living, and he should have died long ago.

"Staring into the sun can blind a man," warned Hemora.

"Solaris would be so kind. My old orbs are cracked; could use a drink of water." His reply called into question his effectiveness on the operation.

"Try being a fish out of water. That'd make the situation worse."

Ignoring his poor health, they silenced until the search met its end; a thanks owed to an unlikely detective. Eventually, it wasn't Haruka's hyperactive senses that found the bandit hideout, or Lucille's tracking expertise, but rather Gerald's inquisitive nature, and Hemora's inability to fully control the steed.

In a spur of frantic galloping, the steed bucked Rick off his back and continued with Harlan alone, over to a small growth of palms by a pile of seemingly unremarkable boulders.

"Hemora, where's he taking me?!" the dwarf panicked as Gerald made his way a fair distance from the others.

"Try and hold on. Gerry's not the tamest of animals." It was an unhelpful warning made with no concern for his safety.

What waited by the rocky landmark turned the plan of attack into one of salvage. Several mangled corpses looked as if they'd crawled from the entrance to a concealed cave. Each body had a unique array of injuries upon them – cuts, broken bones, gunshot wounds – but all bled out recently. Capped off with the stench of decay, it wasn't a bearable thing to observe.

Hemora praised Gerald, patting him on the side. "Good boy. Probably the most competent member of this team. Oooh shit, there's dead bodies."

"Good. Would get boring otherwise," Haruka added, earning a jab to the arm from Lucille.

"Damn. Late to the party, again," Rick said, looking over the rotting ruins. "They're fresh, though. May still catch the attacker in the act. I'd be pleased to dish out some southern justice."

"We're going to talk to them first," Lucille said, clinging to her strict morals even in the heat and the sand. It was this persistence that Harlan admired; more will than most youth.

"Oh, I'm gonna talk, sweetheart. But whether they listen or not is up to them," Rick growled, poorly trying to sound calm and collected.

Hemora refused to join them in the cave – the molluskan's blood-fearing nature was too overwhelming, and he opted to remain outside, on watch.

"Have fun. Don't die," advised the fish, wishing them luck.

Harlan, worried and wounded, spoke out against this.

"We'll need it, given my sorry state." He'd not brokered a peaceful solution to a conflict so heated, and was fearing he'd bitten off more than he could chew.

"If it all goes sideways, I'll happily take centre point," volunteered Haruka, seemingly disagreeing with her friend's peaceful ideals more than ever.

A bitter warrior at a glance, Haruka could prove problematic for the negotiations, unable to partner with a 'master diplomat' like himself.

"You should stay on watch, too. If the attacker bests us, then you'll be a last line of defence."

"No, that's a stupid plan. Hemora can handle that menial work," Haruka denied.

"I don't think so," Hemora regretted, looking paler than usual around the mouth. "I really, really need a hand. Not feeling myself."

"A little batty?" asked Haruka. This was the biggest truth Harlan had seen, with Hemora's fear of the blood making him recoil and shaky, in need of stability.

In a nauseous manner, the molluskan was reduced to begging. "Please."

"Consider it done," Haruka accepted with a sigh. "Only if your retched horse stays away from my poisons. If the foolish foal persists, then I might just let him at them next time." This unnerved Gerald and he whinnied, fearful of Haruka's callous heart.

"Don't listen to the mean lady, Gerald. She doesn't mean it," Hemora said, comforting his horse back to a steady state.

"I do. Lying for others is a talent of mine, but lying for oneself is petty."

"Petty? Good thing I never lie then."

"Really?" she jolted with sarcastic shock, covering her faked, agape expression with both hands. "Batty indeed."

"Ah, it's good to see you *dance* around matters of social importance like this."

Harlan had no clue what the two were talking about, and Lucille looked just as dumbfounded, so instead the elf turned to him.

"After you, Harlan," she beckoned, pointing at the short cave entrance, letting him take the first steps into the dangers that awaited.

The caverns were cool compared to the plains, and the air even had a moisture to it. The walls of the hypogean paths were sandstone, but as they dove deeper, the sides began to become lined with stalagmites. All the time, satin pools of red appeared in greater number, loaning credence to Rick's suggestions of an attacker.

"The mites must indicate water nearby," Harlan said, almost salivating at the thought of a nice lake to swim in.

"Or more bodies," Rick commented.

They pasted by some boot prints heading into the caves, and even a scorched set of prints, encircled by blackened sands. They smelled of charred leather and spice: an odd thing that Lucille remembered from her younger years.

"This doesn't feel right. There's no sign of anyone here except for a few footprints leading out," Lucille said. "I doubt anyone's left down here."

Their talk was overrun by a sombre voice at the end of the tunnels.

"That's because there's only dead men in this cave, girly." Stern words from a sterner voice, and a voice that belonged to an unknown element: a stranger.

"Their goes any element of surprise."

"If it's just one, then we can take him," Rick said back.

"And it could be a trap."

"Could be. Could just be a hermit that we stumbled upon. Let's take it slow," Harlan ordered, and moved towards the stern breaths ahead.

The area expanded into an open room, and even had the lake he desired, sitting defiled at its centre. What had been a crystal clear body of water now ran red with the contents of several more dead men and women. Most were young boys and girls, all reaped before their time.

As with the bodies topside, many were dismembered and mutilated beyond saving, and a couple were impaled on the larger stalagmites to the right of the pool.

The sought-after supplies sat behind the tainted water, and were untouched by the viscera – a respected commodity, even in all this violence.

Lucille was taken back at the image, in shock at the atrocious display of the macabre. She writhed with disgust, and her breaths shortened with each new death that presented itself.

In the middle of all the death and post-carnage was a tall, battle-damaged man, covered in cuts and rips of all sorts across his flesh and clothing. His black coat looked like a torn rag hanging off his lowered shoulders, and the matching cap he bore had several bullet holes tearing it apart. He had bandages stained a dark red winding up his muscular arms, indicating an attempt to halt the bleeding, but a failure that spelt an approaching fate.

Below the torn coat were innumerable straps and belts of black held together with silver buckles, making it all too clear what this man was before the slaughter – the very bodies he slaved over would soon be his home. Who would dig his grave?

The most notable wound was his left eye – or lack thereof – as his orbital had collapsed into the space where the ball should be, with the excess blood and silky grey hair covering his identity. The trio gawked at the man for a while, and Harlan could only speculate what had happened prior to their arrival.

Licking part of the red from his lips, the Stranger smiled at them, and faced their mix of disgust with the broken warmth of hospitality. By pulling a blue handkerchief from his around his neck, the Stranger wrapped the crushed eye he wore, poorly concealing it from view.

"I can see you over there, staring. I'm not blind – yet. First my brother disappears, and now *this*. You here to finish me?" asked the Stranger, battling gravity in a poor attempt to stand.

"Far from it. I'm Harlan Ainsworth, and these are my associates, Lucille Woodward and Rick. I'm here to make you a deal," Harlan answered, as professionally and nobly as possible given the current circumstances.

The Stranger paused, then broke into a heavy laugh that transformed into a fit of harsh coughing, causing him to splutter an unhealthy amount of fluid onto the soaked ground.

"Rick? Just Rick? What, you scared to call him a Greycoat now? There's indecency in such a kind welcome."

Harlan doubted the long-term survival of the wounded man, and his strategy quickly changed from diplomacy to waiting out the Stranger's clock. Lucille couldn't blame him for nature's course, and they could bag the stolen inventory after the cap dropped.

"I met you, back at your last display of cowardice," Rick said.

"I ran, yes. But, well..." Before the Stranger finished, he chuckled more, adding more discoloured mucus and pus to the soil. Harlan didn't see the point; there was no joy in your own death.

"You're finding this too funny."

"Heh, look around you, Harlan Ainsworth. What do you see?"

He thought it to be a trick question; all he saw were the entrails of a great many people.

"Death?" he answered, hoping that the obvious was the answer.

"Correct. Bodies all over the shop. This sanctuary, a promised land that fell short, is now a crypt. I'll join them soon enough, and your friends will pick my corpse clean, in addition to all the others." The bloody

Stranger said this while reaving each breath. Then, the dying man's joyful nature disappeared. "But you will not touch *this one*."

A quivering, pale finger pointed to the Stranger's feet. Lying there was an almost pristine body with only a lone bullet through its skull. The hairy man remained as handsome in death as he was in life; blonde locks of hair and empty, blue eyes stared back at them with conviction.

"Was he your friend?" Harlan asked.

"Once. Then, he was so much more. Now, he is nothing. A vessel of lifeless flesh that used to contain dear Oaken's soul. You *will not* touch it…" The Stranger finally succumbed to rest, sitting on a sandy rock beside the body of the man named Oaken, a man who the blood-soaked Stranger held dear; perhaps even responsible for kicking the whole bloodbath off.

Harlan remembered his own defeat, kneeling by loved ones past. In the moment, grief was absent – only duty remained in the ruins of a family. When duty was finally fulfilled, then grief moved in.

"If those are your final wishes, then so be it," Harlan negotiated with sympathy.

If the gods favoured the ex-prisoners, then that would be all the Stranger wanted. It wasn't.

"Which one of these murderous bigots wanted to deal with you three, anyway? Eh, doesn't matter; doubt old Kit will come looking for his water from beyond the grave," the Stranger wheezed. "Which reminds me, I need my body buried under the sun. If tradition serves me correctly, then my spirit must go on to serve Solaris in the afterlife. I never was a holy man. Let's hope Sol's the forgiving sort."

A sunburned burial was common for those of a certain sect, and Harlan was willing to accept this, until he was interrupted by Lucille.

"Give you burial rites? You've murdered a dozen people, bad people, but people all the same," she said, in disgust of the butchering.

"Sorry, girly, but I have no sympathy for these animals and what they did. Neither should you. People like you, ya care too much for all the wrong reasons." The Stranger reached into his pocket, pulling out an old pipe; one last smoke before the end.

Harlan watched the fearless man stuff tobacco into the pipe, before the numbed hands of a dying body forced the Stranger's pipe to the ground. "Damn, was looking forward to that. Let's hope Sol's a smoker too. Do the gods smoke? Eh, whatever. Do you smoke, girly?"

All the Stranger got in return was a glare of sharp hate.

Harlan wanted to side with her, but this man's dying truths might be just what she needed to break her oddly prestigious morality. He took a step back, allowing them to hash it out. "He's given you the floor, girly, best not waste it."

"I have nothing more to say, murderer."

"I did the right thing."

"What makes murder right? Nothing. You can't just come into someone's world and take something they care about, whether a brother, sister, husband, wife, whatever, it's not worth it," she screeched, throwing sorrow in her speech. "I learned that the hard way."

Still keeping a belittling grin, even amongst all the death and anger, the Stranger turned to Harlan.

"See what I'm talking about, Ainsworth? 'Someone's sister, husband, wife'? Too much time caring about what others think, when the end is so much more. Death isn't always about other people. Sometimes it's a personal and individual thing that's needed, even wanted."

"No one needs death," Lucille snapped.

"Tell that to a grieving widow... I'm sure they'd be happy to end it all. In fact, I know so."

The Stranger was clearly getting to her, recklessly hacking deep to her untapped nerve. Harlan got to see his first glimpse of her darker nature surfacing as she raised her bow and gave an ultimatum.

"What if I killed you, then? Would that be *personal* and *right*? Who'd care about your passing?" she asked, threatening what little existence remained behind the Stranger.

"No one, really. The love of my life is in heaven now, with my parents and brother. All didn't deserve death, all got it, and people like you are the reason their killers sit pretty in prison and not in hell. My death wouldn't be like that, though – it would be euthanasia at best; a mercy killing. Something I believe that even you could manage." Opening his arms, the Stranger welcomed the cobalt arrow that'd carry him away.

"This shindig has to end," Rick said, moving closer to the tension. "You can die here or live in a cell. The choice is futile, and yours to make."

The detective's movements were fast, and caused the Stranger to lash out. A pocket knife, carved from baobab with a tip of silver, came shooting from his coat and cut across the same line that Langdon's rapier had.

"Never interrupt me when I'm teaching, Greycoat!" raged the Stranger. The instant the anger entered them, Rick fell over, gutless again, and the aggression left the pair just as fast.

"Here we go again," whispered Rick, as he slowly faded from the far gone 'diplomatic solution'. This needed to end.

"Lucille, shot him!" he ordered.

"Yes, Lucille. *Do it*!" the Stranger reiterated.

Lucille held the Stranger in her sights for far too long. Her morals were being tested, and he hoped that for once they'd fail. In the upcoming battle against King Barsalt, her morals would need to evolve in order to survive.

"No. I can't do it. Kill when you can kill? It's wrong. Just like you," she said to the man, and lowered her bow.

The Stranger finished teaching and toying as he growled in anger at Lucille's incompetence. He stood back up and spat at her.

"You're not listening, girly. I'm going to tell you one last time, but I'm not going to use my words to do it." Lunging at her, he drew the knife, intent on teaching her the hard way. Harlan, determined to play the hero again, jumped between them.

"Don't do this. Go peaceful–"

But the damaged Stranger had no trouble pushing the dwarf's burned body into the sand, and continued to go for Lucille. The pain of a hundred daggers hit Harlan's flesh as he planted his sore body to the floor and listened to Lucille's high-pitched scream.

Rising from the sand, he saw a daunting sight: the Stranger standing over Lucille, with two cobalt arrows sticking through his chest. Blood from him and the other bandits covered Lucille from her head to her feet, a baptism tailored for the weary wood elf. Her still face said it all – she had danced with the reaper and lived, a woman reborn in the blood of a Stranger. At this moment, Harlan knew he'd made a mistake.

"See?" the Stranger whispered in her ear, as he slumped over. "Kill when you can, or they will instead." He died with a frown on his face and tears in his eyes – from one eye, a trickle of clear water, and from the crushed socket, blood oozed.

Harlan moved over to Lucille, checking her for any wounds. The results were both unexpected and tragic. She had none, because the Stranger had retracted his knife's silver blade moments before; he posed no threat, but she didn't realise until it was too late.

She looked at the weapon, then to the arrows that pierced the flesh, finally throwing herself into Harlan's arms. He didn't know if she needed comfort from him, or if he was just the closest source of warmth in this cold, lifeless cave.

He didn't care about the blood or his burns, for right then, in that very instant, the two had a connection, and it felt good despite the poor circumstances that overshadowed it. As with all his love, Harlan's was cultivated in a bed of failure – one he sought to erase.

Chapter 14: Days Gone Bye Bye

Lucille stayed frozen in fear at what she'd achieved. Not since her arrest in Valordolt did a feeling this rich in disappointment and heartlessness occur. The Stranger lay just like her last kill. Neither made her feel happy or glad, only empty.

Harlan ripped a piece of untainted fabric off her victim's pant leg, and went to cleanse her of the sinful act, wiping away the blood, as if to rid her of guilt. The cloth smelled of him: of the Stranger's bilious musk. It stood as a reminder of the lost life and all consequences that clung to it.

Needing to get away from the man, the corpse, the smell, she pushed Harlan away and forced her quivering legs to move. The slow exit was stopped by Rick, who continued to fight against his wounds for a second time.

"Wa-water," he gasped, from his immobile state.

"Tough isn't the word," exclaimed Harlan. "Lucille, help me move him."

But she refused. What would losing one more life mean today? Rick was a stranger, just like the others; nothing to her, nothing to Hericore's plan, nothing to Magnus' existence.

"Lu!" Harlan called, only to be turned down again.

"I'll live. I'm fine," Rick panted. "She needs some fresh air. Go... Send the others if you can."

Her continued shuffle up to the surface was sped up by Harlan's helping hand. The dwarf disregarded Rick to keep her own broken self moving, all the time supplementing her sore soul with kind words. His support reached her, but rivalled silence in its moot nature.

Right then, she cared not for his or anyone's charitable encouragement; it was the same kindness that placed the arrows in the Stranger's shattered heart. Her kindness forced his charge and then offered him another sort of kindness by putting him out of a prolonged misery. All the reasoning she offered was for naught – he'd received what he wanted, regardless.

As the warmth of the sun engulfed her, she thought of re-evaluating her moral code; an ideological evolution. If this series of events happened again, she might not be so lucky, and find a dagger buried deep in her guts. Losing one's insides was Rick's duty, not hers.

Outside, Haruka was leant against a palm, with Gerald at her side trying to satiate his greed for attention. This ceased when both saw Lucille and her new crimson costume.

The look on Haruka's face was a blatant 'I told you so' look, but she refrained from bathing in self-righteous rants and opted for a more humane approach.

"Glad you two are okay. When we heard a scream, we feared for the worst. Is Rick...?"

"He's okay. Well, dying... but okay," Harlan explained. "You and Lucille should go back home and send help. Even with Gerald, we can't carry an entire store's inventory back."

The wood elf could see through his motives. He didn't need the help – he wanted her to get cleaned up and back to a comfortable place. Honest goals, good goals, but unnecessary. She didn't need comfort, she needed to be on her toes, needed to keep her mind away from the Stranger and the cave.

"No. I'm going to the inn, I need some wine," she said, storming past Harlan, back to town. "Well, Haruka, are you coming or what?"

"Of course."

She pushed past Hemora on her way back home. He stared at her sadness, and she stared back.

"You're right to fear blood. It signals the birth of a monster."

"Yeah? Right. Umm... Harlan needs me, sooo..." Hemora awkwardly said, as he, like all her friends, left her. And now, she was left to bask in the 'thing' she'd become.

***

The trip back was longer than Lucille remembered. That being said, she did have to carry her bloodstained self through the heat, and the burden of the word 'murderer' clamped down on her heart, adding tonnes to her weight.

Haruka kept her distance, for a time. She was smart like that, could tell how bad Lucille felt, and silence was needed.

The Stranger's words rattled inside. *'Kill when you can, or they will instead'*. Why did it have to be so? Couldn't people have some decency for a change? *Blood shan't pave the road to victory,* she repeated, but kept coming to the same conclusion: yes, yes they can.

Though a harsh reality of the world she lived in, Lucille knew deep down that it wasn't going to change. Her life was shaped by this inability for peace to rule, everything needed to be measured in pounds of flesh.

All she could do now was accept it, and watch as the violent abused the passive, the strong abused the weak, and the bad abused the good.

Oh Charles, she thought, *Oh Charles, I've failed you*. A hope lingered that her brother could hear this admission of failure, small though it be. He strived for more, a world without the Stranger's ilk – this meant a world without her. His memory was all that remained of his vision, and corrupted or no, she'd kept fighting for it.

Haruka finally spoke to her wayward cellmate. As was the trend with the assassin, her words were few and daunting.

"You'll forget this one day. It happens to us all."

"What?" Lucille replied, unsure how an event of pure bad could be skimmed over even in time's thick waters.

"People always forget their first. I did."

"And if I don't? If I'm the exception to this rule of thumb?"

"Then maybe you can walk away from this life; realise the errors and run," Haruka said. "Do what I couldn't."

"Maybe. For now, I just want to rest."

If she was going to sit back and watch mankind go to shit, then she'd need a drink in hand. Though not a regular boozer, she was willing to make an exception today. If the Stranger's death meant anything, it was a good excuse to get hammered.

***

The next day arrived so fast. After the alcohol took control, the morning after seemed to appear within minutes of walking through the Bled Lizard's doors. Waking from her stupor, yesterday's horrors felt more like a bad dream – a bad dream that formed into an even worse hangover.

Headaches were an uncommon occurrence for her, which made the present one even more excruciating. Along with the ache came a plethora of fuzzy thoughts, and things became hard to recall. Coupled with a sickly taste in her mouth, it didn't feel pleasant at all. Her hair was in a flurry and stuck to some reddish gunk on her cheek, she had a pretty clear idea what that foul gunk was: yesterday's wine.

The rest of the camp were in the midst of packing up all their belongings, and preparing to move on to the Arcana Oasis. This was a journey she could easily leave for another day; the world's end could wait on a hangover.

Harlan was outside of her gross-smelling tent, trying to shove his pudgy legs into his black iron suit, which yielded poor results. Lucille crawled into the light and allowed it to crack her fragile brain even more. But slow adjustment to the brightness set in, and she looked Harlan up and down.

"You know, if you rolled up your trouser leg, then maybe it'd fit through the clasp," she suggested, her voice croaky and dry.

"Tried that. It didn't work so well." He hammered his fist on a tightly-wound coil that held the ankle clamps together. "Glad to see you're back with us. I came to check on you earlier and you must've still been stewed, didn't even know my name," he chuckled, striking the clamp over and over.

"Could you not smash that? It's doing a number on my head," she requested, feeling a woozy grip on her stomach.

"You sound pretty bad. Need a drink? Of water, I mean. Not wine, that'd be a shot in the foot."

Accepting the offer, she made short work of the canteen, moistening her parched throat and freshening her stagnant breath in the process.

"Having trouble with that clasp then?"

"Yep, this whole thing really is a two man job. Think you could pull it open while I slide on inside?" he asked.

"Sure, just what I need: manual labour. Have you seen H-Haruka?" Despite feeling fuzzy again, she managed to lift the clasp up just long enough, allowing Harlan to wedge his meaty calf into the cold iron.

"Thanks, Lu. Haruka went off with Rangar, 'bout an hour ago. They were trying to find Hemora, from what I heard. Our ladies' man swaggered off with two buxom lasses from the inn last night," Harlan said, before mumbling, "Lucky git."

"Sounds like all of us had to forget yesterday. Me, Hemora, you and... ah damn, how's Rick?"

"Surviving," he replied. "Hauled him back on Gerald, and he's gonna make it, *again*."

"Good to hear. Now, I think I'm going need to grab something for this headache. I'll be tracking down a potioneer if anyone's looking for me."

"Hey, you're okay now, right?" Harlan worried.

Searching for a feeling was harder than it sounds, and 'okay' never came to mind.

With indifference, Lucille replied, "I don't know?"

The group wasn't nearly as ready to leave as she thought, and needing to quell her cranial pain, she slowly marched to town.

Journeying around, her mind cleared, but the memories were still faded. Feelings remained, ones of family and happiness, but the faces had no place. Sure enough, all details on her family were blank; she failed to remember her mother, father, any siblings she had. They all vanished.

Any fear she felt purged them further, and after the brief panic wore away, nothing was left – no happiness or sorrow, just a void. Whatever happened last night was of concern, or should be. But without past feelings, she couldn't have concern. Lucille felt only a calm in her empty heart, and bided her time, hoping this feeling was temporary.

Moving away from the camp, the emptiness persisted, and felt stronger than any old hangover. *I had a family, I know I did,* she thought. Again, only the blankness remained.

"This can't be. What's happening?" she whimpered aloud, checking the horizon, hoping to still be in a dream. Then it happened, out of nowhere: memories started to return. From the void came ones more recent – she felt remorse for murder, anger at herself, and repressions of affection for… someone; it wasn't quite clear. "This is all temporary. It has to be. Some pills might make it better. They have to."

Holding all her self-hatred close, she marched on to the potioneer's with panic in her haste.

Her remaining trip across town was uneventful. The cave bandits must've been the only contention Declandale had to offer.

Philip, Helena, Thomas, and Travis were all in the Lizard having breakfast, or in Thomas' case, a couple of dinners worth of meat. She looked down on such carnivorous gluttony, but it was good to see Travis up and walking, even if it was on one leg. Thankfully he'd pulled through – the world needed good men like him now she'd turned to more destructive methods.

On the opposite end of town was another camp of mismatched tents, and among them was a potion seller, and his business, Pavlov's Potion Palace. It was a gimmick of a name that brought a weak smile to her balanced mood.

Her approach to Pavlov's navy tent was cut short by a bizarre interlude.

"You're not visiting royalty, you pig!" shrieked a women from a tent besides Pavlov's. "You lied to us, you shrivelled squid!"

"I wasn't shrivelled where it counts though… right, ladies?" bargained a familiar voice.

Lucille then witnessed Hemora and Rangar running like wild dogs out of said tent. Hemora was without his shell, clothing or weapon, as he made a dashing escape past her. Rangar was in his wake, hauling Hemora's belongings under his arms, including the shell.

Hemora's actual flesh was remarkably white, almost ghostly. She'd never seen a naked molluskan before, and prayed never to see one again. The flabby and wrinkled flesh under the shell was formless, and sloshed around with his strides.

Lucille was also treated to the unappealing sight below the waist. Suffice to say his arms and legs weren't the only appendages that were wrinkled and flopping about.

"Didn't I tell you? Fish junk!" Hemora shouted at her as he bolted past.

A well-groomed gnome, with a worn suit and novelty-sized pointy hat stepped from the Potion Palace, just in time to catch an ugly glimpse of the commotion. The look on his face instantly matched that of a man who'd seen far too much.

"Goodness gracious. It appears the gods want to sear my eyes from their skull with that display," squeaked the gnome.

"Oh, that's just Hemora – he's a friend of mine."

In a lecturing voice, he replied, "Then you need tamer friends, my dear."

Lucille smiled. "I wouldn't have them any other way."

"Well then... Please step inside, Miss. We're now... open for business," he said, bewildered by what transpired.

The gnome pulled black-rimmed spectacles from a pocket, and a glistening, blue flask from the other. Swigging the flask and placing the glasses atop his head, the gnome beckoned her entrance.

"You're Pavlov?"

"The very same."

She entered his shop just as two – thankfully robed – women chased the lads towards the high street. Though the day was young, her new allies made everything a long haul, and she loved it.

Pavlov took a seat on a book pile at the tent's back, allowing Lucille to pick her potion of choice.

The shop floor was no more than five or six feet long, and the products were crammed together on the poorly-kept shelves. Outside, the bad aroma was faint on the breeze. Inside, it overpowered the senses and made her sickness deeper, causing gag or two.

"Please, no expulsion of fluids on the wares. I've learnt that lesson the hard way," Pavlov said, to which she politely obeyed.

"It's quite alright, I came here queasy. I'd bet even a field of flowers would turn my tainted stomach."

Though cramped, the bubbling of a few cauldrons could be heard along with the fizzing of a soda distillery. Such a flurry of noise confused her drunken head; the Palace was an assault on all her senses, and she couldn't find their origin. "Bloody brilliant," she further gagged, clutching her mouth, "let's make this quick."

Instead of buying a pre-made concoction, she opted to buy the cheaper, individual ingredients, and brew the draught herself. Her family memories were elusive, but her knowledge of herbalism remained.

As she picked out the fullest otten flowers and most potent darkfruit, she heard Pavlov's mumblings across the room.

"Must move back home; too many revealing troglodytes here. Bloody naked molluskans, the audacity."

"Again, Hemora's a friend," she reminded. "Trust me, he's a very special case. The rest of the town shouldn't be put down for his 'unique' personality."

"Don't worry, m'dear. I'm moving on anyway. It's just one of those days," Pavlov said, as he rubbed his temple in a tired manner.

"Ain't that the truth."

She came over and placed a bunch of ingredients on the counter: otten flowers, darkfruit, mint, and powdered mushrooms.

"Ah, brewing away a night of drinking?" Pavlov questioned; his deduction skills were impressive.

"Do I really look that bad?"

She may have cleaned off the upchuck, but her hair still remained unkempt.

"Not at all. But in future, may I suggest an alternative to liquor?"

"Go on..."

The gnome pulled the half-empty flask back out, and relieved its top.

"This can work miracles that alcohol cannot." The potion smelled familiar, but like most things that day, eluded her. "This is Ale of Amnesia: potent, and popular amongst youths," Pavlov yammered. "Why, last night I sold one of these to a girl of your vigour."

"Good to see I'm not the only sucker around."

"It wasn't for the girl. Said her friend needed to forget her awful day. '*Everyone forgets*', she said. Funny isn't it? Whether potion or pint, we all need to forget some things. For me, it was that aforementioned molluskan," Pavlov tattled away.

Everyone forgets? She thought on this for a time, before the words connected to a soft easterner's quote. '*Everyone forgets their first*'.

Her blankness sparked into an inferno of thoughts, leading to an unfortunate end. She then knew who this mystery girl was; the only girl that could care enough to steal her memories.

"Thank you for those words. I won't forget them," she said.

"What words?"

"I think I'll need to talk with this customer," she told Pavlov, leaving him and his ingredients behind.

"I'll just put these back then."

She didn't listen to the gnome's complaints, too livid over her suspicions. Determined, she marched away, hell bent on interrogating Haruka. Being one of the closest people on this mission, Lucille felt a deep sickly feeling of betrayal in her body – worse than any hangover. How could Katowa do such a shady deed?

Not two minutes after leaving Pavlov's tent, Haruka intercepted her.

"Have you seen Hemora? Me and Rangar split up and are trying to find H–"

"The boys can wait. We're gonna need to talk about your little visit to the Potion Palace," Lucille interrupted in an aggressive tone.

"Nothing much to say. I helped Philip pick out a few things, and picked up some poisons for the road ahead." Haruka was a convincing liar. Too bad the truth already reared its malformed head.

"Really? Because I was just talking to the owner, and he told me a different story."

Haruka's expression turned sour; Lucille matched that look, and their long-lasting chemistry began to rapidly break apart. The pair began to sizzle, slowly leading to an inevitable explosion.

"I just thought I'd help you with yesterday's little problem." It was a sorry explanation that wasn't taken as gospel.

"So you think I'm too fragile? Too prissy to handle it?" Lucille interrogated her, keeping on the offensive, not willing to let herself be held down any more; times were changing, and so was she.

"Can we get out of this heat? It can make blood boil more than it should in this type of situation."

"No. I want you to tell me, right here, right now. What makes you think you can change my life – *my memories* – without my permission?!" the elf pushed loudly, drawing the attention of everyone on the high street.

Haruka paused before answering. Both could sense the amount of friendship that was on the line here, and neither wanted to hear the wrong answer.

"Lu, you're a nice person. Back at Refracted Light, when Jantell used to scrap with you, you'd always take the hits instead of hurting her back. You'd rather let yourself take the pain than let another suffer. That sort of kindness and innocence is hard to hold on to and impossible to regain. I just wanted you to keep it for a little while longer."

"So you admit to what you did?"

"I never went through with it, I swear!" Haruka lowered her voice. "I can't do that to a person I… *like*."

She didn't know how to respond. Haruka had never said anything so thoughtful in the year she'd known her; that kind of emotional heel turn must mean something. An all-out attempt to hold on to someone you can't afford to lose, maybe?

But it still did not excuse the theft of memories; not to her.

"That won't do?"

"What won't? My sincerest apologies?"

"No, the apology was welcome. It still doesn't excuse the act," she said. "My past wasn't yours to take."

"I didn't take them!" Haruka prattled. "I couldn't do it, and I won't repeat myself again."

With condescending words, Lucille spat back an equal response; achieving nothing but a steady flow of bad blood.

"Bullshit. I still remember yesterday, but I can't seem to remember anything from before this horrid life we're living. Only the pain remains, Haruka. Lying is okay, isn't it? Long as no one lies to you."

"I speak the truth. I'd never lie to you," Haruka said, her voice softening, and her eyes puffing.

Both girls were losing their emotional constitution, racing each other to eventual tears. But Lucille remained red, unable to remember many things: her home, her brother, even her crimes. Whatever dose Haruka gave her was too much. Larger and larger gaps in her memories formed, it terrified her.

"I can't remember him. You're lying to me, right now. You're lying again and again, you two-faced *bitch!* No wonder Helena hates you. And after what you've just done, I'm amazed that you're still able to sleep at night."

Haruka turned away and had nothing else to say, her tearing face looked foreign to Lucille, but sadness wasn't any good now. She'd been robbed, robbed of all the wrong things; the Stranger's words weren't one of them.

Kill when you can was a mantra held by all the killers in her life: from Haruka to the Stranger, and now herself. Unable to kill Katowa, she did the next best thing.

"I never want to see you again," Lucille warned. "Take your murderous, cold heart, walk into the desert, and DIE!"

"Lucille... I..."

"No! Leave me and this cause you so desperately hate. Not for *one* second did you care about any of this, or any of us. We were all just a means to your selfish ends."

Taking the advice with no resistance, Haruka left, along with any support she gave. Lucille watched, as her last best friend stormed off into the distance, doomed to be taken by the sun. She felt only one thing: regret.

Chapter 15: The Potion Palace

Philip was sour. After all he'd done in the pursuit of his dreams and their success, Hericore had relegated him to another run-of-the-mill lackey. This building storm of ill choices would soon catch up to the drake, and he was now more than happy to watch.

Sitting on the fence was a vulnerable position to view the world from. When fence started to shake, the fall was soon to follow… and what a way to fall.

News of Haruka's departure was also a hard hitting reminder of Hericore's botched leadership, and Philip was tasked to find the reason why she left.

He and Helena combined efforts, and quickly found a 'why': Lucille admitted it was her. Only the 'how' didn't quite make sense, and their new task was to tie some loose ends in the whole incident.

"You must miss her. You and Katowa got on like two pips in an apple," he joked.

"Yes. As close as you've become to Kenneth."

"Hey, my ideas aren't unfounded," Philip said confidently. "Our pal Kenny suspected Rick: wanted him gone. Now, the Greycoat is laying at Lilith's door again."

"A coincidence?"

"No such thing. To a man who can see the future, there's little faith in lucky happenstance." This comment was far from the current truth. With his visions faltering, the future was again a free-for-all affair.

"And what have you seen of Kenneth?"

Helena was close enough to confide in over the visions, but never so close as to inform her on their diminishing appearance. Another night passed without a flicker of what was to come, and it was a fearful prospect for Philip.

"Nothing special so far," he fibbed. "He loves to dance around those sands with sword in hand, though. Take from that what you can."

"You don't believe in luck. I don't believe in swords."

"Each head holds a philosophy. Some are more progressive than others."

"And where's this head leading us?" Helena said, wrapping her arm around his shoulders, and gently pulling him closer.

"Lucille claims her memories have gone – a lot of them, at that. Haruka could've bought a bad batch of Amnesia," he answered, pushing away from Helena's grasp.

"Smart," she complimented.

"Don't expect anything less, plum."

Before they could reach the herbalist, Lucille came bursting out of the Bled Lizard, drunk on something other than alcohol, though wine still played a crucial part. Her cheeks stained with tears and her eyes uncoordinated, she was in a terrible way. It was unbefitting to see discord in the strong elf.

Harlan followed her out, a virulent watcher through it all. Ainsworth deserved a break, and maybe he'd find it in Lucille's bed one day. Cats often staled a bird for hours prior to pouncing. Harlan had waited far longer than that.

"Evening crew," Philip saluted.

"Go fuck yourself, Philip," Lucille replied.

"Wow, that was rude. How much have you had?"

"A couple."

"Couple of bottles," added Harlan. "Sorry about this, Phil."

"It's okay. We've all been there."

Willing to do the unthinkable and forgive, he'd forgotten how reckless grief-stricken people could be.

"No it's not 'alright'," Lucille defied, slurring all the while.

"Isn't it?" questioned Helena.

"Yeah, *Smelena*. Because you'll never guess what I just discovered." Before either could answer, Lucille did the honours. "This world – Karin, *Midgartt*, *Magnus* – shit, all of it. The whole bloody planet, and everyone on it, are just *terrible* people. That's okay though, 'cos if everyone's terrible, then I don't feel so bad now, aye?"

Philip admired the way she thought. If all it took was a few drinks to make everyone that accepting, he would've turned alcoholic long ago.

"Good on you, Lucille. Now why don't you go back to camp with Harlan? The big kids have some business to attend to," he said, trying to distance himself from her potent breath.

"Big kids? Helena maybe, but you're a joke," Lucille taunted, swaying around him and replicating his smirk. "A spineless pencil-pusher, trying too hard to play leader. Surprised you've made it this far on an inflated ego."

"Is that so?" Philip humoured her, his rage building slowly.

"I know so. There's a reason Hericore and Rick don't like you. Hemora thinks it's your inability to stand your ground without Thomas there. He's not wrong – but I'd also blame all that charisma you toss around; a poor weapon of choice. A coward's arm."

Harlan tugged on her shoulder, ceasing her bumbling argument.

"Let's go, Lu. You're not acting yourself."

"Well then, if I'm not *myself*, then I should just do this..." She then turned and clamped her lips to Harlan's for a solid ten seconds, disregarding her heated argument. The dwarf's fists tightened – as did other areas. The whole time, Philip could hear Helena's light gagging from behind.

"Let us go," Lucille yelled, throwing her arms around and staggering away. But Harlan stood there, stunned, only moving when she pulled him away.

"Bloody brilliant," he said in a haze.

The pair moved on, but Philip had one last message for her – one of warning.

"And, Lucille," he called, "one day, men that push pencils will rule this planet of filth. Best to keep in their good graces, pumpkin." With a delayed salute in reply, Lucille took Harlan away into the night.

"That was mighty sickly," Helena said.

"She'll sober up eventually. And without the past to hold her back, she'll be stronger than ever."

"Why? Is that one of your dreams?"

"Nope. Lucky guess."

"Let's just hope she doesn't remember what just happened… for her sake."

They moved off the high street to a compact blue tent with a curtain for a doorway, lined with smooth, golden silk. A mixture of smells diffused through the curtain, reminding Philip of foul rotten fruit, blended with sweeter odours of mint and lavender; typical signs of a potion seller.

"Pavlov's Potion Palace? Pretty tiny palace if you ask me," he said, examining the quaint exterior.

"Don't judge a book, honey. Remember that dwarf back in Valordolt? The one muscles bigger than your head," Helena reminisced.

"Of course I remember. We paid him to arm wrestle ol' Tommy. Shame his mighty guns snapped in two. No smith on Magnus can fix those kind of weapons," he replied. The two chuckled in the glow of a thing so morbid.

Helena was a woman, but never a lady: a trait that Philip fawned over. She was a refreshing contrast to his last flame, entertaining his desires while being exotic and erotic at the same time.

"Ladies first."

"I'm no lady," she corrected.

Philip originally thought the small tent would be a ruse, and the owner had enchanted it with an illusionary compression, making it bigger on the inside. He was wrong.

Yesterday's visit was a lone venture, and he prayed Helena had a similar distaste for the Palace. Indeed she did, and whispered this in words of disgust. "It sure is cosy in here."

"Too cosy for my tastes."

The shopkeeper was a stout gnome who sat on a pile of books, but even then, he was no taller than four feet from the ground. His face was crumpled and his finer features were lost amid the creases in his skin. Wearing a smoking cap, the gnome had the appearance of an eastern lord, having a formal look and a sickly-sweet aroma.

"'Ello there. Welcome to Pavlov's Potion Emporium," said the gnome in a high-pitched voice that both Vagabonds found it hard not to laugh at. Gnomes had always creeped him out, and this one was no exception.

"The sign said 'Potion Palace'," Helena nitpicked.

"Indeed it does. I'm currently going through a bit of a marketing crisis. I still need to change the signs. The economy these days, am I right?"

"The whole world's on a diagonal. What's new?" Philip agreed.

If Hericore's ramblings held any truth, it was that the end times were near. Days shortened, nights became darker, travel was a hazy venture, and even the passage of time felt subjective. This was why Philip had allied with the drake, for what little good it did him. The world needed a hero, and he wanted to fill that role.

"Indeed. I'm Pavlov, at your service, in health and sickness, for today and the next."

"Save the speech, chief. I've been here before. But I'm not here to buy enhancers or Morphos; this time I want answers."

"Answers? Of an alchemical nature?"

"No. I wanna know what junk you mix into your Ale of Amnesia," he accused, "Your mix erased my friend's memories."

Haruka purchased the Ale, and regardless of who popped the cork, Pavlov must've sold a faulty product. He, and by extension, Hericore, would settle for no less of an answer.

“Yes, I remember. That was the purpose of the Ale – she did realise this?” Pavlov said.

“Naw. *Really*?” Philip replied, acting in a goofy voice. “I thought it'd make people fly. I guess with a name like 'Amnesia', it can be pretty misleading.” It was a long, tiring day that he wanted to see over, and the only obstructions were Pavlov's dumb questions.

“Apologies, sir.”

“Damn straight. Now, what's in the Ale? Ya thin it out with water or something?”

“The recipes are a company secret,” rejected Pavlov, “I can't tell–”

“Can't tell? Or won't?” Philip said, stepping closer to the humble gnome. The little blighter was wise to withhold secrets, but not from him.

“Hun?” Helena said, holding him back. “Calm it. We're here on Hericore's behalf and should represent him.”

“If we represented Hericore, we'd never get answers.”

Even while sleeping, the drake's inadequacy hindered him.

“Whatever happened to your friend, it wasn't my brew. A foreign toxin was introduced *before* consumption,” said Pavlov.

“A foreign toxin? What, like a poison?”

“Of sorts. Ale of Amnesia is a rather delicate mix of elderberries, concord shell, and pines, all fermented in–”

“It's hard to make. We get it,” he furiously cut short.

“Any manner of chemicals could offset the intended effects. That is all. No taints, no corruptions, and certainly no thinning.”

“Well then, case closed. That's that. *Findante,*” Philip dismissively clapped. He knew the exact source of Lucille's plight, and all that he needed now was a face to blame.

“I'm lost,” Helena said.

“Me too,” Pavlov added.

“Well, that's a good sign. The less clued up you are, the better. Thanks for the help, half pint. My darling and I need to discuss matters not suited to your little ears.”

"Philip! that's not a nice thing to say," Helena scolded.

"Not nice, but apt," he replied. "That reminds me. I need some more painkillers, chief. Head's a mess lately."

An unamused Pavlov frowned.

"What happened to half pint?"

"I say stupid things when I'm being clever. It's the best weakness I could've ask for. Now chop chop," Philip ordered.

Shortly, Pavlov pulled some green-tinted pills from under the counter and stated their price.

"Four roths. *Each*." The heavy vengeance placed on the word, 'each', spelled a weakened wallet for Philip.

"They were three roths yesterday."

"Yes, and yesterday you had manners, sir," Pavlov remarked.

With muffled curses, Philip handed over a small pouch of bronze coins. Pavlov looked down at the bag from his seat upon the books; there was no way the gnome could reach, just as Philip hoped. He wanted to see the gnome struggle to grab the coins: it'd give him amusement, at the very least.

Instead of meeting the challenge, Pavlov pulled a bronze bell from a satchel to his right and rang it five times. The echoing chimes resonated through the tent and beyond, until a puff of pink smoke shrouded the counter. Once it cleared, a chimp, no bigger than Pavlov himself, appeared out of the pink cloud and grabbed the pouch on the shopkeeper's behalf.

"Nice trick," Philip said spitefully. "Does he get paid in peanuts, or what?"

As Pavlov counted the money, the gnome told the history of his little simian friend: their start, their trails, and their triumphs. Philip didn't care for his story, and regretted his snide comments. Gnome voices were insufferable.

"All the coin is accounted for. You have enough for five pills; use them well. I'll be leaving town soon, and I'm the best around."

"I'm sure you are. Safe travels," Philip wished as he walked away. But upon leaving earshot, he added, "and good riddance."

***

The sun was gone from the sky, and the moon ruled in its place. With it came a cool stream of wind travelling across the flats, towards the town. Taking a seat inside of the Lizard, Philip ordered Helena a flagon, and himself a cup of warm milk. With the drink, he swallowed a handful of the pills, and hoped for a sound skull free of throbs and stabs.

Helena still looked troubled, and had been for days. In a desperate attempt to avoid his fatherly interrogation, she babbled together a string of small talk. Talking with such a tiny scope made him uneasy; everyone did it, but no one wanted to. It was suspicious more than anything, just a distraction from a person's true thoughts; a verbal iteration of his mask.

"Travis saved me, you know. Langdon wanted to dice me up something fierce. I'm glad he only lost a leg," Helena rambled, with half a glimmer of admiration. Philip had gotten the impression she didn't care for Travis' nobility or loss, only the convenience of his rescue.

"Kid's lucky he's not dead. And I'm not sure he feels the same as you. Most guys just love to give their limbs up for a pretty face," he doubted, quickly moving from one Vagabond's suffering to another's. "Now what's it you wanna vent about, plum? And don't lie. I'm rather used to that sulk of yours these days," he asked, while they drank.

"It's nothing."

"No, it's something. Else you would've taken my advice and smiled."

It didn't take much convincing for Helena to loosen her lips – it never did.

"Well, you know your visions? Have you seen anything of *him* in any of them?"

Philip had to think for a moment to deduce who 'he' was. When he realised how stupid the question was, the tone changed, and the air gained a coldness to it.

"Helena, your pap's dead. You made sure of that last time we were in Karin. Seven chest wounds don't just heal themselves. And in the middle of the desert? No one could've saved him," he said, shooting down her worries.

"And if someone *did* save him?" She still clung to her bad memories, all the ones that scarred her, both physically and mentally.

Her dad, Vince Starr, had a prestigious title around the desert lands, but that was in reputation only. Philip brief encounter with the man behind the title was nothing short of pure disgust. She was lucky to escape him.

"What's gotten you all worked up over him?"

"I saw him near town, not long after we arrived. Stalking me from camp to water pump and back again."

"You saw his face?"

"No. Just that horrible suede mess he liked to wear. And that gun plastered to his hip..." she replied, looking down at her treasured pistol Love and losing her focus.

With fear dripping from her sides, Philip knew Helena's mind needed settling. His closest and brightest ally couldn't work like this.

"Then you didn't see him. You saw a man dressed like a frontier walker and were reminded of him. Post traumatic stress and stuff. Nothing but a wild idea put in motion by a bad memory," he said, rationalising what he could.

"I want to trust you, but for now, can you tell Tom and Travis to keep an eye out for him?"

"Sure thing, plum. I know how tough these messes can be, especially for people like us. Just keep calm and don't worry, okay?"

"Okay," Helena smiled.

Their drinks were swilled down, as they watched the moon rise high over Declandale. The blue hue around the buildings was nice on the eyes, and the gentle howl of distant creatures soothed their coupled minds of grief.

"Today was long and full of pain. But tomorrow will be... much... better," Philip said, in a failed attempt to sound deep and reassuring.

"Nice philosophy there, Archilleos. Somehow I don't think that'll land in history books," she joked. Talking was a trait Philip had in spades, but not one he could muster at will. The best speeches he'd ever given came from depths that were unreachable day-to-day. Fear, pain, the end… all were emotions perfect at drawing out the best in him.

"I can't be on point all day, babe. Not that I'd like to be."

"Now it's my turn," Helena said softly.

"To do what, exactly?"

She took his hands and placed them in hers, gripping them loosely. They were alike – both hiding, using masks to lose themselves in a kinder reality. On occasion, his mask would slip to reveal a sad boy beneath it. Helena made it her mission to avoid this, for everyone's sake. Life was dimmer when his smarmy grin flipped upside down.

“I was distracted by a ghost from the past. I can tell you're worried about one from the future.”

“Close, but missed the mark. It's the present that's got me miffed,” Philip admitted.

“Hemora's insults were a crude attempt at humour.”

But that wasn't the reason, and he grinned.

“Hemora's a punk with a lot to learn. He's harmless. It's Kenneth that troubles me.”

Helena stared with a confused gaze. “Seriously? He's more harmless than Hemora.”

“I hear him whispering when he thinks no one's listening. To top off the psychotic behaviour, he wants to learn how to fight – desperately so.”

After accepting her burdens – making them his own – Helena failed to do the same. Disrespect was a second nature to him, but when it came from her, it slighted him more than anything.

“Don't we all?” Helena said.

Philip bristled. “Hey, I listened to your wild problems.”

“By calling it just that: wild.”

Her words were quick, like her skills with a firearm. But his were steadfast, and it'd take more than wit to wear him down.

“Why was he in Refracted Light then? Kenneth is dangerous. I'll prove it.”

“The person that spiked Lucille's ale is the real threat.”

“Kenneth could be both our problems. Dangerous, and toxic,” he replied, attempting to kill both birds with the same accusatory stone. “At least he’s an obvious scumbag; not like ol’ Hericore.”

“You’re turning on him now too? I thought we’re supposed to protect him?”

“That’s what I thought, until I started thinking... What if it’s all a lie? He’s obsessed with the Stones; he used to basically lay with the Time Stone back in the day. Do you think that’s normal?” Philip’s eyes narrowed with every word he spoke. His voice became more agitated and sounded like he was going to yell his next sentence.

“I–” Helena tried to break his stride, but was interrupted immediately.

“I think he’s faking it: the curse, the prophecy, all of it. He wants the Stones for himself.”

Helena put a gentle hand on his warm arm. “You weren’t there, Phil. While you were off having fancy dinners and parties with the Order, I was stuck watching that drake spew plague and bile all over the place. He’s sick, at the very least. We can’t turn on him now; not after he’s helped us with so much.”

It wasn't the best feeling, knowing that even your partner disbelieved you. But keeping on, keeping on, Philip chose to forget Helena's frown, and changed the subject to a lighter field. Pulling all the black jokes he could from his sore head, he got to work making Helena smile again.

Like the good old days of the Vagabonds, the two laughed like children for the next hour; slowly eating up what little fun time they had left. She'd say the most romantic things. Whether it was '*I'll always be there for you*', or '*you were always there, even on my darkest day*', it didn't matter. Praise was praise, and he craved praise. His laughs felt more forced than ever, each one made to prompt Helena's next bout of thanks. This, laced betwixt the droll jokes, made for most their conversations these days. Things would change upon reaching Yellemette; for better or worse.

The humour had to die in the end, and the faces of the end were made of shell and scale, respectively. Philip looked out the window to see Hemora, Rangar and Harlan strolling over to the inn, presumably for their own drink and laugh.

"We should leave. If I have to put up with that brutish bunch getting all hands-on and stuff, I might just cry. I swear all those fools have done is drink like bloated bankers while we do the real work."

Helena didn't argue. Philip held a certain hatred for those too enamoured by the bottle, and it was a hatred few stood in the way off – Helena included.

"Long as we keep a few dozen feet from that perverse dwarf, I'm happy."

They left and only had to suffer through one quick conversation with the others. Philip liked their brawn, admired it even; a life he never had the luxury to live. But his innate hatred of their brains – or lack thereof – kept him away.

The prisoners would eat themselves eventually. All crime did was make them hungry; a gaping pang that couldn't be stopped. When all the food was gone, they would eat those closest to them. Not longing to satisfy the hunger pangs of his barbaric allies, Philip kept them all at arm's length, and looked forward to tomorrow.

In his mind, the worst of their journey was over. An arm over his girl, a lack of cut-throats out to kill them: things were looking good. It was an observation that was far from the ugly truth. Philip's mask was about to slip – the optimistic hero was soon going in favour of the sad mess within. History was doomed to repeat itself. All he could do now was take pleasure in the finer sins Magnus had to offer: greed, pride, and with Helena in hand, lust.

Chapter 16: Hound Dog

Kenneth persisted; his practice was surely making him perfect, albeit slowly. With each and every swing, his form tightened and improved. The burns in his frail muscles were soon replaced with the pumping of blood – his body was returning to normal. Twenty years of waste was being re-written, and the man he used to be was returning.

Xander taught miracles, displayed deftly by Kenneth, and even impressing Rangar with his flair and speed. But even with his newfound expertise, another mountain still needed to be climbed if he was to run into Hart again – *when* he'd run into Hart again.

The Warden was known for his relentlessness with a sword, and years of serving on the front lines had hardened him more so. Comparatively, Kenneth was still a bud to his mighty bloom.

The camp was rather barren – with Haruka gone and Lucille inebriated, only he remained. Xander was another absentee, still engulfed in exposing the darker side of Declandale's detective. An absence so long was bound to yield insidious results.

Philip returned with Helena cradled beneath his arm, but offered nothing in the way of communication. Blocking all of his waves and whistles, Philip retreated to a tent; a strange lack of talking for the dandy boy.

After Rick had dismissed and further dishonoured the boy, Kenneth was not surprised by being given the cold shoulder. Making enemies of them all, Rick was playing a rather high-stakes game with the Drakeguard, and Kenneth wanted to be the one to catch him out.

Loneliness failed to grace him much more, as Xander came sprinting home with a worried look on his ethereal face.

"You need to follow me," the ghost said, shocked. "I found out what our coated fellow's been hiding."

With no time to waste, Kenneth darted over to the remnants of Rick's shack in Xander's ethereal footsteps.

"So what is it? What's this shitbird got hiding in his closet?" the old man huffed.

"He's dead."

"Dead? That's no surprise, he was gutted twice over."

Obviously he was missing something, as Xander halted for his idiocy.

"No, I mean he died years ago. But he never left for heaven nor hell."

"That's impossible, isn't it? Unless he's a ghost like you," Kenneth asked, struggling to understand Xander's meaning.

"Not at all. He could be a vampire, or a nasty piece of patchwork. I once met a hag who could stitch two dead together to make a living hybrid."

Neither smart nor shady enough to study under the Black Grimoire of the Dead, Kenneth's knowledge was lacking here. But, uninformed or not, he didn't want to accept the truth of an undead Rick. Where he grew up, undeath was the stuff of legend; the Order cast out the living dead centuries ago, and in this rare instance he actually sided with the Order in this fight.

All those who defied the rules of life weren't worthy of it: a belief he'd had since childhood. Fond memories had been stripped away in Refracted Light, but the nightmares still remained; dark dreams that would never die. In these dreams danced a man wrapped in a velvet curtain of necrotic light, and haunted the child within the lowly fisherman forever – or what seemed like it.

"That's bizarre! He can't be..." Kenneth began.

"You are talking to a ghost. Am I not bizarre?" reminded Xander.

"You never plagued my past; those undead do," he countered, leaving it at that.

Up on the overlook that Rick called home, they found the detective fumbling around the ruins of his shack, desperately cramming all he still owned into a suitcase.

The sweaty Greycoat packed away his iconic attire, unbuttoned his now stained shirt, and left his tie loose as a noose around his skinny neck. For a man recovering from a fatal wound, he was full of zest, practically gliding from burnt corner to burnt corner of the shack.

"Going somewhere, detective?" Kenneth asked, causing Rick to jolt violently.

"Ah, Kenneth. You scared me half to death."

Tired and anguished, he cut to the chase.

"Only you can't die. Can you?" Rick didn't care for the accusation, and finished packing. "Why run? Hericore wouldn't care, we're already a strange bunch as it is."

"You weren't the only one to discover who I am. Hericore knew this, just like that! He was the one to suggest that I run, before the Order finds me," Rick said, with a lump in his throat. "They don't take too kindly to the... uh... 'defiers of life'."

"Nor do I," Kenneth replied coldly.

Ignorantly avoiding his threats, the Bloodhound continued to sniff out any remaining notes and memoires. Clutching a new handful of stitches over his stomach, Rick was pained, but not in any danger from wounds so egregious. The sliced flesh wasn't red nor gangrenous green, with only a drained shade of purple marking each empty vessel.

“I'm not buying this. If he's a patchwork, then the Order should have no quarrel with him – they’re not dead, after all. Ask him if he's heard of Madame Osiris,” said Xander.

“Madame Osiris, is she the one who made you... well, undead?” the fisherman passed on.

At that point, Rick snapped into an angered state. Grabbing him by the leather collar, the note taker set the record straight.

“Get one thing clear, pal. I'm nothing like those freaks that Osiris cranks out. I have an air of class to me.”

Kenneth grimaced. “So you *do* know her?”

“Unfortunately, and that's where I'm heading; to tie up a little unfinished business.”

Kenneth couldn't tell if this admission was genuine. If it was, then his worries were unfounded, and Rick wasn't the traitor. If it wasn't, then he'd be letting the enemy exit unopposed.

“Hericore said you should go?”

“Yes. Twice over since my second gutting,” Rick answered, sounding honest enough.

Many people looked to their leaders for guidance, and Kenneth was no different. Using what he'd learned from Hericore thus far, he accepted Rick's plight, keeping an eye of suspicion on the slick detective.

“Well, I can't stop you. Even if I wanted to, how could I kill a dead man?” he reasoned. “I wish you well, Rick, because no one else will.”

Rick paused, and relinquished the tight grip he held, allowing Kenneth to back away, slowly.

“Same here, Ken.” The Greycoat then stepped in close, and gave one last piece of advice. “I know who you are. The Regatta Ripper,” he said with a great amount of sympathy.

“That was a baseless arrest–”

“I know. Any Greycoat would say the same. Poor investigatory skills all round,” consoled Rick. “But that's old news. Knew it the second you spoke your name. I only know one Kenneth Porter in Refracted Light, and he *should* be rotting in a cell.”

“You’re *the* Ripper?! And you call me a dead man,” spluttered Xander.

“Yet here I am.”

“When Hart finds you, he won't have the mercy to kill you,” Rick warned. “He'll drag you home by the collar and watch as old age takes its course.”

"Maybe that's what I want," Kenneth replied.

"You would reconsider as you slowly feel those growing muscles turn to mulch, and the lightning left in your soul is grounded by your decay," Rick advised in a reflective tone that was too sinister to quantify.

If not a patchwork, then the curse that bound Rick must be similar to decay; a life of rot. The sympathy now flowed from Kenneth, not Rick. Sharing his woeful fate, he moved away, casting off all advice.

"I'm handling my destiny from now on. To hell with Hart," Kenneth said. The detective's warning was outdated. Hart's cruelty was all too familiar to him now.

Giving him a solemn pat to the back, the undead Greycoat headed out to face the desert winds. Like most undead, he showed off a yellow belly and dodged the Order's scorn. If only others were smart enough to do the same.

Turning back once more, the Greycoat lent him a final morsel of wisdom.

"You don't like me, Ken, that much is clear. While the feeling's not mutual, I can't say the same for a certain troubled child we know. Watch your back, and keep him in line."

Philip was a smart kid, and this seemed like one final stir of the pot on Rick's part. Maybe Hericore was wrong. Too late to stop the detective's disappearance, Kenneth waved away the undead with empty farewells.

"So Hericore trusts him," he whispered to Xander. "Hope he's a good judge, else Rick will never face his due jury."

"Hericore's not a too bad, you know? He was the last member of the Drakeguard I met back when he formed the group, in the wake of Palmer."

"You were at that castle where they found the Time Stone?" he asked, finding it a little too convenient.

"Yep. It was just me and Krell back then, wandering the world. It was awful lonely in those days, with nothing but a madman to talk to. After Krell wandered too far and was captured by some vampires, we spent four months in a locked cell until they showed up and sprung him." Xander chuckled at the memory and said, "I suppose we share a past in a cell, you and I. My stay may have been permanent if Hericore's crew didn't roll through the place. I've been shadowing the Guard ever since."

"You must've learnt a lot about them."

"A little. But that's not important. What is important is that you're the Regatta Ripper," Xander diverted.

Initially, Kenneth didn't reply. That title was a hideous scar on his past, not worth bringing to light. This silence was broken fast. Though it scarred his past, keeping it hidden was tearing apart his present.

"Hart likes to think so," he admitted. "Foolishly so, might I add."

"You killed *a lot* of people. Hell, you offed his family too."

"No. I was there, but I couldn't do something like that," Kenneth said, finding little comfort in his words. "Though I can see why he doesn't believe me. The evidence was damning."

The grieving Warden based a trial on nothing but emotions, an unstable foundation that manage to hold for twenty-five long years. Innocent to the world, Kenneth felt nothing but disgust in the face of his conviction.

"I'd swear vengeance on the bastard that damned me for decades. I'd end them and their kin," Xander said. "Though the Ripper did that for you, in the Warden's case. I wonder if that counts as irony, or perhaps reverse irony? You'd be seeking vengeance on that which caused your downfall in the first place… a paradox, maybe? I should know all about those by now; the Guard has manage to caused a fair few paradoxes in the past."

"Irony, paradox, I don't care. I wouldn't want those years back – I'd waste them. All I want is to know who the Ripper is, and why they framed me," Kenneth replied; a simple goal with an impossible journey.

That was all he told of the Ripper, for now. Past pain was best dealt in passing moments, and the moment had passed.

***

The walk back from Rick's place was another streak of quiet.

"A man of few words, aye?" Xander asked.

Too long had Kenneth stewed in his cell, which rusted his conversational abilities to a sluggish crawl.

"I just need a while to get back in the rhythm of life. Hart wasn't the best of hosts."

"You should see his table manners. All doom and gloom with him," the ghost gossiped.

"You followed him, too? Quite the traveller."

The town was dead this late in the night. Only some of Hemora's cheers from the inn filled the air. It was peaceful, if not cold. The chilling winds of Karin took some getting used to, even under his thick jacket. It was equally chilling to be wearing this jacket. Belonging to Xander, it gave a sense of misplacement whilst draped over his old shoulders.

"Indeed," Xander continued, "but he's lost to us now. The next time we cross him, it'll be for the last time."

The camp wasn't as quiet as Declandale proper. Hericore was still awake and subtle moans crawled out from Philip's tent; the kid knew how to keep a good time going.

"Have a relaxing stroll, Kenneth?" asked Hericore. He was resting on the sands like dog, with crossed legs and his head on the cross. "The way you left worried me slightly."

"S'all good, Sir. Just needed to stretch the ol' sea legs."

"That's a lie if I ever heard one. Rick's fled north, hasn't he?"

"How did you–"

"I've spent hundreds of years on this planet. Philip calls me a 'coot', but I know my way around people's heads. I could surmise Rick's condition the moment he returned from death a second time."

If the drake knew, then why keep it from the others? Perhaps Kenneth was too trusting of the Guard, and this tainted his thoughts on the matter. Trust was in a very short supply after twenty years of being caged up.

"Then you also know what he thinks of Philip," Kenneth replied.

"Who doesn't? Youth comes with many perks, and few drawbacks. One such drawback is emotional frailty. Philip is a good kid with good intentions. I feel he's been… we've all been stretched a little too much on this journey." Wisdom flowed from Hericore's beak, and some of it was sobering to hear; all until that sobriety was ruined. "Kenneth, would you mind joining me for a drink of mead?"

"I… um… Are you sure that's wise? Given your curse and all."

The drake laughed in a sickly way, and stopped to cough midway through. "I may be dying, but that is unavoidable. Mead will only lighten my dark outcome."

"Go ahead. You *did* promise him a chance to talk. I'll just wander for a bit; maybe sneak a peek a the 'happy couple'," Xander said, before strolling off with a forced 'ha!'

Without ever agreeing, Kenneth was whisked into the crimson tent. It still reeked of infectious, burnt skin coupled with herbs and spice, but unlike outside, it was warm. Travis relapsed into his slumber after a brief few hours of feasting. Though missing a leg, the kid had a comfortable set up of pillows and quilts. Maybe it was time to lose a limb too.

Hericore's fine claws grabbed a pair of tin cups and a bottle of Brown Barron: an elven brew, seen rarely out in this part of the world. Though the taste was too bitter, Hericore enjoyed it; he called it a 'slice of home'.

"I admire you, Kenneth. If I was in your boots, I'd have given up and bit my tongue a decade back."

"Thanks. Not many people have really cared for my imprisonment. I vaguely remember the first few weeks. It was all rallies and riots for my hanging. I was wrongly imprisoned, and the people didn't want my release, but my head."

The memory of that first week was a faded one. Back when he'd had no beard and only stubble for hair, Kenneth had a bed, window, and more. Hart still had a piece of heart left, and life was bittersweet compared to what would follow. The rallies and riots stopped after a few more weeks; people just forgot how to care. The Ripper's victims gave up on justice – justice for him, and for the dead.

"If it means anything, the decision to charge you as the Ripper was put down to a vote."

"That so?" Trust the broken bureaucracy of the Order to vote on the innocence of the innocent and still come to the wrong conclusion.

"Yes, Hart and the old High Council voted. Three to two was the result. I was one of the two that voted in your name."

"Again, thanks. Even fewer people actively fought for me back then either. Who was the other?"

"Oddly enough, the sourpuss of a banker: Mabel Dirk. I think it was more out of defiance of Hart's wishes than support of you."

It was nice to know people cared, but somewhat worse in knowing how close the trial was to being in Kenneth's favour. After more mead, the night was coming to its high point, and so was the fisherman's exhaustion.

"Why call me in here? We could've talked outside," he quizzed, and Hericore was reluctant to answer. But, after realising how open he was being, the drake caved to the question.

"I'm planning on calling off the mission."

"What!" Kenneth's reaction was so large that it almost woke Travis and spooked Gerald, who was saddled up outside.

"Shh… This is a big decision, and I want to keep it behind closed doors."

"Why? We've come so far; we've done so much."

"That's why it must end. I just wanted to do the right thing. One life for that of the world. But now? Now we've accidentally blown up my home, killed my people, and thrown my Order into chaos."

It was true; the Guard was a growing party of dismay. But among all good causes was a rough patch. He argued this, but the drake didn't listen.

"And what about all the things we've accomplished? You stopped time!" Kenneth emphasised. "I have to admit that was one hell of an introduction."

"A flashy welcome bought at the cost of an innocent old man, tricked into playing a hero. I barely knew him; he was neither friend nor family, and yet I miss him. The world may live a little longer, but was that a toll worth paying?" The drake stroked the banner upon his breast, feeling the charred edges – lukewarm, ready to ignite again. When the next a flame touched them it could be the end. "I've lived nearly a century under the Order, breaking and building all kinds of bridges. Yet, here I am, facing the biggest challenge of my extended existence and hardly anyone believes me. Ish did, and now he's dead: sacrificed for 'the cause'. Sometimes the world seems all too empty."

Kenneth gave him a level stare. "This is your conscience kicking in, ain't it?"

"And yours has not?"

Kenneth stopped and stared blankly. He didn't feel anything about what had happened, other than his own fears. Did this make him heartless or driven: compelled to push on, regardless of sacrifice?

"We gotta keep going. If we stop, then all that's happened – good or bad – will have been meaningless," the old man insisted.

"That sounds akin to Hart's old philosophy."

"Persistence is the one thing me and Hart have in common. We'll keep pushing... because we've both lost so much." Revelation hit, and Kenneth's words became heavy in his throat. Hart was just the winning side of the same struggle for persistence. "We keep going, for those we've lost. I've lost, and I'm not gonna lose again."

Hericore also had a heavy voice, and after finishing the mead, he looked regretful.

"I wish an 'old coot' like me still had that drive, my friend. You've lost too much, and have grown to live with it. I can't do the same." Opening the tent's flap, Hericore showed him the door. "Get some rest. I'll wait till we've found Haruka, then we'll go our separate ways. You're all free now; it was wrong to force you into my service."

Mixed with a rage likened to Philip's, and the permission of Rick, Kenneth walked away with mixed feelings. All of a sudden, the heartless fisherman felt a deep sense of valour for Hericore's cause. Not for the drake's safety, but for that of Magnus. If the curse was unleashed, that would be it. This was the most sobering thought of all.

"You know, I'm starting to feel like a canary: now that the cage is open, I doubt I'll fly away. From marriage, to Hart, to you; maybe freedom isn't in my nature?"

"I spent my entire service to the Order trapped in a cage, so take it from a 'coot': you'll accept freedom not long after it accepts you," assured Hericore, who was now stretched out like a tired puppy. Xander's first talk may not have been too buried in rumour; it did feel like Hericore was peeking into his soul. This wasn't an intrusive look, like Thomas had, but one of warmth.

"Goodnight, Hericore."

"I wish you the very same. May your dreams be ever white and free of fright," rhymed the drake, and with a hollow yawn, he dropped his scaly head.

The night had been eye-opening for Kenneth, as he found an unoccupied bedroll and took off to sleep. However, it didn't come quietly. Long past Philip and Helena's groans and moans, even further than Hemora's sloppy return from the Lizard, and only when the sun rose did his doubts disappeared in exchange for some winks.

Today blurred into tomorrow, and with it came a breath of fresh air. The freshness soon became tarnished by blind justice. Rick was a suspicious man of fluid allegiance, but gave accurate advice when it mattered most. If only Kenneth had paid it any mind...

Chapter 17: The Hunted

Hart held Kalsec's words close throughout his team's recuperation efforts. Two days of rebuilding passed, and on the third, his appetite had left him. Sitting bewildered in the torn and bloody inn that had housed joy days before, the Warden looked around their sparsely-filled table with a hopeless pout. Fit for eight companions to show their bibulous selves, only three occupied it in a display of shivered glory.

While eating breakfast with his captains, he played around with a plate of poorly-fried eggs, refusing to feed the guilt inside. Hunter suffered in the medical grasp of the sole priest who remained alive after the slaughter.

The ringing still lingered in his ears, each bell cataloguing his mistakes. Nothing about the paladin's frenzied nature was animistic, and was almost patriotic, much like the bell's chime. The Order held many secrets, and he didn't doubt the bells were one of them. Lud and the others had died for nothing but Kalsec's desires, and that was only the start of his problems.

More importantly, he hated eggs, or at least the yolk; yet there they sat before him, ready to be devoured. He carefully ate around the gooey embryo as he forced the whites down his gullet.

He once enjoyed breakfast with his family, but that was a luxury he could no longer afford. Countless conversations about this and that would accompany his morning meal. Ray's latest fishing trip, or talks about Chel's favourite breed of pony; anything to keep them smiling. The days may be gone, but the memories lived on with crashing exuberance. In the end, wasn't that all that mattered?

"You know that the yolk's the healthiest part, boss," Boyd said. The large captain made a habit of cramming his food down – bacon, eggs, and even a plate of tomatoes, all vanished in minutes.

"Boyd, which one of us is the superior?" Hart asked in response.

"Err... You, boss?" Boyd failed to understand the question's sharp point.

"Well, when you are the superior one day, you can lecture people on your dietary *opinions*."

Boyd didn't frown – in fact, he smiled and asked with optimism, "Do you really think I could lead some day?"

Hart knew this to be false. The captain's recessive nature, paired with his poor decision making wouldn't bode well for any future career advancement. Captain Loyce was forever the underling.

But he praised him otherwise; the last thing he needed was a disgruntled right-hand man, lugging a sense of worthlessness around the wilds.

"You may have to lead soon. The world's moving too fast for me these days," he bleated.

Boyd beamed at him. "Don't be so down. The prisoners won't outpace us, and they certainly won't best us."

"Look around, Loyce. They already have," moaned Jelz. "I've lost my shot at Hemora, all thanks to that sharpshooting *banca-boyse*. Can't believe you let him walk, boss."

"He limped and panted – barely walking. Watch yourself, Jelz. Your position in my ranks is based on good faith, not reliance," Hart said, holding back any kind words.

Jelz held up his hands. "I'm loyal, don't get me twisted. I'm just pissed off."

"Whether loyal or not, you still chased Hunter's skirt rather than my own. Such a lapse next time will not meet my mercy."

Jelz was a tracker, and that was of great use now, but the Warden would pick teamwork over talent any day of the week.

Breakfast remained unfinished, as one of the troops, a mechanist by the name of Elise, came over to the table. She took the attack well, regardless of the death toll and panic, she kept a blithe appearance. Not a ragged, blonde hair or cracked face of foundation was to be seen; the image of calm.

Hidden from last night's chaos, her cream robes stood dirty and scuffed beneath a blackened leather apron. The girl was resilient, and still had the lingering stench of horse dung hanging around her petite body. Stables were a great places to hide, but came at a hygienic cost; a nose as dainty as hers shouldn't be privy to smells so ugly.

Being the prison's chief weaponsmith, Elise's current job was to find out where last night's attacker had acquired his tools of destruction. This lent her no time to mourn the lost, as with many of the Fork's workers.

Carrying Kalsec's history under her thin arm, in the form of a navy-bound tome, she bowed to Hart and showed him a symbol within the duty book. The marking was of a bare tree under a crescent moon, reminiscent of the Arcwoods' sign: a green-leafed tree rooted firmly in a land of pink, arcane soil.

"Warden, I analysed the weapon Kalsec brandished in your skirmish," she said, through a curtain of draping hair. "*It is* of dwarven origin, of course. But, specifically, it is from a place north of the Ivory Helm."

"There are few dwarves left that far in the mountains. Only the truly reclusive remain. This Kalsec must've made the journey to them."

"Yes, I believed so, at first. But it wasn't that simple. The symbol, it's a trademark of the weapon's manufacturer: their brand." Elise paused, making him edge her forward to a trembling conclusion.

"Go on. Spit it out."

"The marking is that of a hybrid workshop, ancient in the world of smithing, formed by wood elf settlers in the north."

Hart's eyes widened. "He used some old relic to kill my men?"

"Yes. The Celestial Woodsmen fell to an economic collapse over three hundred years ago. It was Fifth's End, only twice as damming," Elise lectured.

Records made up the backbone of the Order's knowledge, and became rather blurred after the past century. Whoever made Kalsec's blade was long gone.

"Relics have little meaning to me. We can't trace a dead manufacturer," he replied, disappointed.

"My examination didn't end there. Reviewing your account of the mechanisms and joints involved, it shows that the whole blade is no more than a few decades old."

"Could be a man out of time. Wouldn't be the first we've faced," Boyd suggested.

Given all the evidence, Hart still had a fragmented view of Kalsec. An experienced man he was, but a traveller of time? That was yet to be seen. Dismissively, he shivered.

"Can't be. Time travel is but an anomaly. The only way through time is forward."

"Is it? We know Hericore's bunch can warp time – freeze it. Could this shadowy assassin reverse it? Phase through it, like a ghost?"

"I said *no*. I will not entertain the queer notion of 'time travel'."

Opinions were built on experience. Unless he'd seen it first hand, Hart wasn't a believer in time travel, or any other stupid claims of legend.

"What we gonna do about this 'traveller'?" Jelz then asked.

"Nothing."

"Not even tell the Council?" Jelz replied, worried. "He commanded their knights, killed them all–"

Boyd broke this talk with a sickly reminder, "*We* killed them all."

"Right now, Kalsec isn't after us – he let us go. The fiend must have opponents elsewhere, which means the old adage, 'the enemy of my enemy', is in effect. We'll work separately, obliviously to each other until our paths must cross again," he settled, placing them far from Kalsec's long reach.

Jelz, again troubled by the reply, went to speak against his rule for the second time that day.

Moments before Hart was barraged with more criticism, the Fork's last priest came bursting into the room, with wrinkled hands coated in Hunter's young blood. Wiping his moist brow and removing a tiny monocular from his sunken eye, the priest held news of subjective relief.

"Sirs, I am happy to report Hunter's splendid recovery! The lucky sod's breathing again. And I believe he'll survive his injuries."

The table let out a triumphant cheer–all except for Hart. Bethany must not favour him after all, instead sparing Hunter, continuing the reign of lesser men. Or maybe it was just another test, one of higher dedication to the cause, and if he needed to succeed, then Hunter's head was the price.

He wasn't above murder – not in the name of goodness. Bringing back a horde of prisoners? That was good as can be.

"Smashing work, Doc. What happens now?" asked a relieved Boyd. "We can't just leave him here; the boy spared us from the block."

"Most of us," Hart added, before plotting a new way forward. "I've got it under control. Take me to him, Doctor." The decision was quick, and his molluskan captain made this even clearer.

"Sure that's a good idea? He's probably not even awake."

"What did I say about giving out opinions, Jelz? I need to debrief him on what happened, and why he's not going to walk again. Not a fun task, but one I'm obliged to undertake." Holding a scornful voice, he made a brutish exit, leaving his subordinates to eat.

Feeding his guilt stopped him from enjoying breakfast, but after this, he'd never fast again.

The Fork's folks were quiet after the attack, and he didn't blame them. Losing your sense of safety was a terrible experience and would continue to plague the settlement for months; such was the way of life.

Elise followed Hart to the medical hut. Keeping hold of the Grimoire, she was urgently awaiting a moment of privacy.

"Warden, I need to tell you something else – an addendum that you *need* to hear," she begged, stricken with a fearful look.

"Cheer up, Elise, we won," he reassured her.

The assurance was meant more for his own sake than hers. Kalsec had left him a tick that fed on misguided feelings of worry and shame.

"You're not taking this very seriously."

"I've been serious for too long. The days of my cheer have long since departed, but now I have reason to reintroduce the old me." But the girl didn't know him, and failed to understand his story. In plain words, he re-phrased the speech. "Make it quick."

An eagerness to finish what he'd started with Hunter grew, supplemented by Kalsec's tick, and bred under a new found freedom from order.

"The blade you described is a marvel of an age gone by. As a designer, I'd give blood and bond to see its inner workings. But, as a servant, I must warn you. The blade's looks aren't the only thing to pique my interests."

Elise struck him as a woman of elegance, a trait coinciding with Kalsec's form, and by extension, his equipment. His sword was beauty made metal, with a punch to back its allure. Elise had the beauty, but lacked a punch of her own.

"The sword? What of it?" he asked, maintaining a dutiful expression.

"Sword? No, that description is a disgrace to the majesty of the blade. That is *the* Moonsabre, a signature of the ultimate night-stalker."

"Kalsec did love the dark. But I doubt it was by choice," Hart replied offhandedly.

"No, the affinity to night doesn't define who wields the sabre," Elise insisted, breaking into another history lesson. "It's said that he who can wield the sabre – a bright streak of light shining in the darkness of man – must too be a vessel of such contrast. A person of both light and dark; neutral, for lack of a better word."

Neutrality was a disgusting display on Hart's moral compass. Life was a gambit of decisions; most were doomed to make the wrong ones. Those who claimed the neutral path with a standing coin flip only delayed an inevitable bad decision.

"Nothing about him was neutral. That man had an agenda beyond you and I."

Elsie frowned. "But his work *is* neutral, even if he doesn't agree. All who fall to him fall by need, not want. A balance of life and death is made on the Moon's sharpest scale."

All the talk of legends and the Moonsabre meant little to him – until the mention of balance came to light.

If those struck by the sabre were bound for death, then he'd be dead. But death never came, and only a nick to the flesh took its place. Hart and his captains were meant for something more. Legends were the fever dreams of man, but the gods' will was final, an absolute that all must follow.

"This proves it," Hart said sternly.

"What? This only proves that your head has evaded death; an evasion that can't persist," Elise replied, puzzled.

Hart set his jaw proudly. After a week of chaos, things were starting to take shape again. "No. I must truly be favoured by the Goddess. If her hand hasn't helped me this far then who else has? Now if you'll excuse me–"

"Wait. What about Kalsec? Your mark. It's still to come, you're cut, he's judged you."

"Yes. I accept that. But not now – I'm required. Another fell to Kalsec's hand before I did. And if you believe in these stories, then I have a job to do."

Cheating death was nothing new to a war hero. Only the 'heroic' could survive a battle, and Hart was used to displaying such heroism. If legends truly had power, then the end would take him, but if they were nothing but a thin mirage of smoke, then Kenneth's hide would wither in Refracted Light for all eternity. All Kalsec managed to do was speed up his downfall.

"What of Hunter? He's the other marked man," Elise asked, reaching a terrible realisation of his intent.

"What of Hunter?" Hart replied menacingly, and entered the priest's tent alone. It was time to prove Bethany's unspoken word, while simultaneously and ironically fulfilling Kalsec's bidding by collecting the Moonsabre's mark.

The credibility of legends battled higher callings, and all relied on relieving his crippled comrade from duty. The boy deserved more than being a pawn in the greater game – they all did. The grim truth still remained: whether he believed in gods or kings, both still played him for a fool.

The hut was a sterile environment constructed of stone bricks and full of soft, cotton furniture. Though clean, it was a cold place, the persistent downpour didn't help. Breaths became vapour and were exuded at a faster pace. The bedding was thick wolf's fur, stuffed with the overused cotton, smooth to the touch, able to hold back the cold.

Hunter lay flat on his back, with an array of powders and creams on his wound to keep out infections and further injury. Bottles of red liquid were lined up on the bedside cabinet, three empty while five remained full. These contained concentrated blood, used as an expensive but portable alternative to a transfusion. If Hunter wasn't receiving the blessings from Bethany, then odds were he was kept alive by these bottles of slowly dwindling vitality.

The wood elf's face was pure white – on the extreme end of weakness. A stiff breeze could end him, and given the weather, it wasn't unlikely. If he had his way, Hart would make sure a calm suffocation would lull the reckless fighter into one final rest.

Suffocation wasn't the noblest of deaths, but a clean and quick one; more than the boy deserved after usurping Hart's authority and leaving him to rot. Hunter was maybe doing his job, but that was no excuse. Hart had lost far more by 'just doing his job' before.

The creaking floor woke Hunter, and it didn't take long for the kid to acclimatise to his condition.

"My legs, they're dead?!" Hunter shrieked, with realised sadness.

"Kalsec wedged a shot right where your spine ends. Not even prosthetics will help you now." Hart broke the news with his condolences.

Hunter had no cunning comebacks – not this time. All the kid did was sob, quiet as a whisper. Losing your faculties wasn't uncommon in his line of work, but Hart disliked seeing the effects, all the same.

In wars past, he'd done the same; some kids were even younger than Hunter. "Chin up, kid. You're one tough bastard," he calmed, but Hunter wasn't relieved.

"Kalsec did this?"

Amnesia was common after dipping in Etheriam's pools. It'd be a miracle if the kid could remember the slaughter at all.

"Yes. When I showed up, the coward took off."

"This day was long coming. Knew he'd bump me off, ever since I was rescued from Palmer," Hunter said, moping with repressed conniption.

"You're still breathing, aren't you?"

"For now. But the legends don't lie. I'm marked now. Should have been the second I joined our *precious* Order. The whole council's a bunch of half-wits… except Wellington, who holds but a quarter wit." A coughing chuckle left Hunter's lips, and even caused Hart's stone face to crack, bending his lips into a small grin. "Wow, guess it really is my last day on Magnus; the deadpan Hart cracked a smile. But seriously, Ryon's a moron, Clara's weak, and Dirk…"

"Go on."

"She's up to something, she was barely fazed by Belmont's destruction. I was ordered to make you a straw man for the whole thing. Reeks of conspiracy; I've had my share of those."

The kid's honesty was admirable for a man of equal honour. Hart had tossed that notion to the wind back in his cell; Hunter's words only managed to let the cat out of Dirk's bag. Nothing was going to quell his motives, but it did make a good excuse to quell Hunter.

"If you helped cause Belmont in anyway, you've betrayed all you once fought for. If you're marked, then death awaits you," Hart reminded him in a suggestive tone.

"And like magic, there you are. My own personal reaper," Hunter said, raising a limp arm to create a weak introduction. As expected, he was a smart lad, but that was no good to a hunter; those of speed and reflex left no room to think.

Quicker than he awoke, Hunter fainted in a sweating mess, but no lapse appeared in the boy's breath. Death was yet to come.

"You still with me, kid?" Hart asked, shaking the boy's shoulder. With no response came an opportunity to finish this sad story, Bethany's will be done. "I guess you deserve an explanation before I put you down," he said softly to the unconscious Hunter. "Tuck in, kid. Tuck in, and I'll tell you the story of Hart, 'The Hapless Fool'."

Like a rhyme told to lull a child, he wrestled Hunter to rest with a story steeped in more reality than Karl the Kraken or the Trapmaster. "You're known for your lack of worry, fear, and guilt; not a care in the world. So I don't expect you to understand what it's like to lose a loved one. Hell, I don't even think you have loved ones. But imagine you did, and all the pain was traced back into one man. One – tiny – man."

The story's villain came to mind, and the Ripper was all that was wrong with the world. A beast in leather, a bearded full-stop at the end of all life's sentences – the longer Kenneth lingered, the more Hart feared him.

Welling up, he finished. "What monstrous things would you do to make sure that man was punished for all that pain, all that sorrow? I may be a monster to you, but I have my reasons. Which is ultimately why you have to die; you're unintentionally keeping that man from justice," he told Hunter, pouring his heart out, unloading his emotions onto deaf ears.

With a tear forming in his eye, Hart took the next step into becoming the vengeful monster he knew was rising, and removed the pillow from under Hunter's hairless scalp. From disobeying his allies, to betraying their trust, to killing them in their sleep, it was a slippery slope, but one he couldn't avoid.

Once Kenneth was back in the Prison of Refracted Light, then maybe, maybe he would turn himself in; maybe then the world would be short a few less evil heads. As he held up the plump pillow, Hunter's eyes peeked open and weak words formed.

"You're one psychotic fucker. You know that, Percy?"

"You heard that? Strong as ever," Hart admired. "I've got to do this. It'll be me or Kalsec. I pray Etheriam is good to you."

The boy knew it to be true, and a sigh served as permission. Holding back sadness, replacing it with tenacity, Hunter said goodbye.

"Bethany teaches honour and love. We're neither loving or honourable, so please be truthful. I'm a dead man either way. Kalsec caused this, but you're glad it happened, aren't you?" Hunter asked quietly.

He owed Hunter the truth, but it was a debt best repaid later – far later. A man's last moments should be peaceful, whether friend or foe; the Wastern Wars had taught this to him, ten times over.

"No, through all the grief and denial, I lost myself, kid. I don't hate you, nor do I want to see you dead," Hart lied, before diverting the subject. "Heh, it's funny. I doubted you even prayed to the gods. Guess we're not so different."

"I never needed to till today. My actions were my words, and my prey were my prayers. I sent them to Bethany, not words. But now, all I want is a place in heaven, and without prey to offer, my words must suffice."

Hunter stopped, and dropped his voice into a more remorseful state. "I lived a good one, that much is clear. From whelp to warrior, hunted to hunter, I ruled this corner of Magnus best I could. And you were right, Percy: I never held love in my heart. But I still had friends, and I failed them." Pausing in remembrance, Hunter closed his eyes. "Pebbles, I'm sorry. And to the boys of Rysin, I'm on my way."

It was a touching farewell that all men deserved, yet weren't offered enough these days.

Hart sighed. "Again, it's me or Kalsec. And I'll pray for you."

"Go on then, do it. I lived for the hunt, the ferocity, and the adrenaline. How am I supposed to do that with limp legs? I've nothing without them. Kalsec has won, and I won't stop you," Hunter said, accepting his fate. "But I'm not the one who needs prayers, Percy."

"I know," the Warden replied, as he lunged downward, and pushed with all his might.

Hunter did as he said and didn't resist – not that he could after all the blood loss. It took almost no time at all to drain the last ounce of energy from the hunter and send him off to Etheriam. The kid was free to a land full of forests and fields; a paradise awaited the determined youth.

Bells rang in the distance – at least that's what Hart believed. They plagued him, a taunt that took a dastardly form.

Closing his own eyes, he saw the Ripper, ringing a chime with as much weight and resonance as the mighty chords of the Cathedral. The Ripper laughed at the dead hunter, and further at the Warden's misfortune.

"Rest easy, Warden Hunter. Pray for me," Hart whispered, before placing the pillow back in its place, wiping away his tears, and calling in the priest. Hunter needed burial rites, and he needed repentance.

Leaving the tent behind, he stepped into the dim light of Rainfall's noon – it didn't blind or burn, but felt wrong on his skin.

Over the horizon rode a contingent of paladins, answering the Fork's cries for help. A dozen riders, a black carriage and a barred coach made up the contingent, the latter vehicle brought for him.

The captains and Elise ran outside to meet and treat with the paladins, but it was no use. The Order loved to hold sway in the land, and knight-slayers like themselves weren't going to walk easily. All he could do was take a bullet for his comrades and scheme all the while.

"Boss, what do we do? They'll kill us all."

"No, Loyce, they'll kill me," he calmly assured him. "As for you three… 'Code Black' may be your only option."

"But my wife–"

"Take them to the Vault, if you must. Do the same for Elise; the girl deserves a port in the storm we'll unleash."

It was a risk, placing so much faith in Boyd, but his list of allies was thinning by the day. The Code was drastic, but if the times matched...

"Mr. Hart, what a pleasure to see you!" called the lead knight, striking a fair resemblance to Lud in build and appearance, however, he wore silver plate from the east. "Shame you're not in the cell Dirk left you in."

"My apologies, but, I had some lose ends to tie up," Hart said, preparing to malinger on the darker side of the law.

Foulness and discourtesy stuck to his ego before, and they wouldn't now. Conjuring a fake air of disappointment, he stepped forward and faced the knight with a puckish look.

"Such as?" asked the knight.

"Like killing Hunter and his boyish scouts. And since they tried to stop me, I butchered the paladins too. Glad you showed up. I was about to add my captains to that list – maybe have a quick pound on this weaponsmith's… ugh… *pink anvil*." He lied with open arms, begging for arrest.

And he got what was desired so dearly – the paladins lobbed him in the cage and hauled him back home. A circle of wasted time formed, for a time, but it would all be corrected if Boyd played his part. Faith in man always made his favour, and he'd never play anyone for a fool.

From Hart's cage, the clearing rain gave birth to a mighty burst of sunlight. A small reprieve, but needed all the same. He felt warmth, and with it came absolution from all sin.

A hunt ended today, but like the change in weather, a newer, brighter one began.

Chapter 18: Breakdown

Philip sat with Travis at the mouth of his tent, looking out north to what they'd left behind. The Vitalands were nothing but the past now. It was never a homely land, just a holdover until he could return to his real home – or what would be his real home.

Heat was a foe stretching back to his childhood, but a small gripe for the expansive land of Karin. This arid sea of orange was full of threats, some closer than others. It wouldn't be long until they travelled deeper into this hell, and he'd be a step closer to paradise.

Everything was moving on as planned. Lucille and Harlan packed away their belongings and Helena was winding down from an active night. Love held little place in such a lustful time.

Kenneth still practised – all the Ripper did now was practise, and this unnerved Philip to no end.

"Do you think the guys will find Haruka?" asked Travis.

"What, the dimwitted duo? Unlikely," he shrugged. "Rangar couldn't find his ass with a map, and Hemora.. well, Hemora's the very meaning of overconfident."

"Rich words coming from you," the cleric retorted.

"Sure, my confidence is a little... inflated. But, I'm not an ass who abuses such power."

If the past was any indication, then he and Hemora were more similar than he cared to let on. Confidence, if nurtured improperly, could make a man powerful beyond his controlling limits. Philip, however, had no time for limitations.

"Really?" Travis asked.

"Yes. I'm certain you don't have a leg to stand on here, pal," Philip quipped. It was met with a glare, but a worthwhile one. "How's the stump holding out, anyhow?"

"Itches. 'Nurse Lucille' said not to touch it though, so I suffer the irritation," Travis said, gazing down at the forced limitation.

"Nothing new there. We've been suffering irritants for days now," he mocked. "And now they've scared off our best killer."

Haruka was no easy loss. She was almost a deal-breaker in the plans to stop King Barsalt. All she amounted to now was another chalked up defeat. One in a long line, by his standards.

"If she's gone, does that mean the plans have changed?" Travis queried.

"Gods no. You think some ninety-pound chick from the ass-end of the world will change all we've worked for? *Please.*"

"That's not all we've lost. Daniels sent me a pigeon; we've lost Hunter. People are saying the Warden got to him."

Having a bald lackey to misdirect the Order's burning scorn was nice, but never important. In one of his early dreams, Philip watched the religion's golden heart mashed to a pulp under a god's mighty foot; the Order would fall to chaos one day.

"Then we move on without his help. We'll just have to work hard and study harder. A kingdom won't crumble to muscle; it'll be our minds that win the day, pal. More important issues have my attention now, anyway."

"Like what?"

"Me and Helena think Kenneth's the traitor who sold us to Langdon, his brother, and the entire Casterland," Philip said, releasing his secret theory to another set of ears. Like Helena, Travis shrugged it off as superstition.

"'Tis nothing more than the hot blood playing tricks on you. Finding faith is key for our success. We lose faith in each other, and it's all over."

"Now who's talking out of line? You've lost your little 'connection' with Bethany ever since your leg got lopped off. Faith is blind to us both, pal."

With puppy dog eyes, Travis looked inwards for a witty reply. The cleric often tried to stand on Philip's own level of confidence, but he made sure to push the bookworm down with as little scorn as possible.

"I've not lost her grace. It's all a tad hazy right now, much like your misplaced fear of the elderly Mr. Porter."

"I'm serious. He talks to people when he thinks we've looked away – he whispers to them. It's much like you and your Goddess, only it feels so much more… real. I feel eyes on me, Travis, and not the usual belittling stares. This is something more ethereal, something more." He repeated the spiel he'd told Helena with twice the gumption. All the doubt was getting to him. Kenneth hid a great guilt, and he'd prove it.

***

For the better part of an hour, Philip observed the fisherman from afar. Finally, after fifty long minutes, words mimed from the old man's mouth. This proved it; Kenneth had made contact with someone, somewhere.

Again, he waited and witnessed a second talk, then a third – he wasn't allowing a fourth.

"Travis, back me up."

"I can't even walk. Can it wait? You're being unreasonable," disagreed Travis.

"Your job's to aid me, not bicker."

"No, my job's to aid *everyone*. That includes the old man."

Philip wasn't impressed. With a quick grab, he held Travis by the robes, and warned the pure fool of his line stepping.

"Call me wrong once more, and I'll make you crawl across Karin. Is that understood, *my humble servant*?"

An unintentional burst of hatred flew through him, and he retracted the verbal claws from Travis' neck before an answer was given. Instead, he marched over to the training traitor and gave him a piece of his mind.

Philip was mad, not lethal, and chose to ditch his dagger before facing the fisherman head-on. Hericore tolerated many loses, but would never harbour a self-made psychopath on the team. He wasn't just sheathing his arm, but also his worse judgement. Besides, the image of blood never sat well on his hands.

"Kenneth Porter! What in all that is holy are you doing!"

With a confused look, Kenneth answered with speed.

"Training. What are you doing, Phil?"

"My duty to protect this group, this mission. Who are you speaking with?" Philip firmly posed.

"You?" replied Kenneth, not losing his innocent façade. A smart mouth would only save one man, and Kenneth wasn't him.

"No, who were you speaking with *before* me? When you were 'training'."

This dark tone drew the attention of Hericore, who, as usual, stuck his chipped beak into business beyond his jurisdiction.

"I talk to myself sometimes. I've mentioned this before. I've got my share of bad habits, kid," the fisherman responded, all while retaining a cool head.

"Oh, you do? Conveniently, it's when other people's backs are turned. Who are you working with?" Philip repeated.

"Break this up, Philip. Whatever you think is happening, it can be discussed civilly," Hericore intervened.

"I'm working with *you*, Philip," Kenneth wearily said, opening his arms to displaying the empty air around him. "There's no one here."

The dandy stepped in real close and gave a final chance to Kenneth, a final shot at admittance. As patience declined, anger rose, cracking his weary facade.

"Wrong answer, you little *shit*," he seethed. "Is it a ghost? A telepath? Is it the Trapmaster that you're working with?"

"Calm it, Phil. Now!" Hericore said, diving deep into his own pool of boiled blood. A dragon's roar could freeze you in fear. A drake's roar could chill the spine. But a dying fool's? Such a fool had no fear attached.

"All I want is a name. Who's the architect building the Guard's destruction?"

Timely silence wavered, and a response without a name would project regret. He'd find regret in leaving his worse judgement behind.

Kenneth's ears perked up, and shortly, he gave an answer, "Philip, there's–"

One jab to the gut silenced the reply from Kenneth's mouth.

"A name!" Philip demanded, over and over again.

The Drakeguard and prisoners all crowded from a distance and watched, as Kenneth remained still, with only a single hand quivering on the grip of his sword. "What's the matter, Cap'n?" Philip taunted. "Too scared to answer? Been found out like your little pal, Langdon?"

"Not at all," Kenneth explained, angered and gruff. "I'm just trying real hard not to cut you down, kid."

A mutual void of sound hit the pair; silence took hold. Then, with a roar, Philip tackled his target down to the sands and a brawl followed. Kicks, punches, and throws tied them together in a show of bruised flesh and cracked bone. Helena called out to Philip several times as she attempted to close in and end the fight. Hericore pleaded for diplomacy and peace, but there was none left to be had.

"MURDERER! TRAITOR!" Philip boomed in Kenneth's ears, all throughout the inelegant dance.

Harlan and Lucille huddled together and witnessed it all unfold, onlookers to the fisherman's unmasking.

Kenneth may have been an old wreck, but like most life, he still contained an animalistic drive. Kenneth's drive gave him the advantage, especially against Philip's own lacking strength. Changing up tactics, the dandy tweaked his combat style to dirtier moves, from kicks and punches to an onslaught of eye-clawing and groin-stomping – several bites were also thrown in for good measure.

"Can't be a man, even now!" Kenneth insulted. "You're pansy ass is long overdue for this beating!"

For all his insults, it didn't win the fight, and another stalemate was drawn.

"Take them down! Break them up!" Hericore ordered Helena, but she wasn't a fool's soldier anymore.

"No!" Philip cried, pulling back from Kenneth, to her side.

His humble concubine held her whip in one hand and Love in the other, leaving him with a single option. He ripped the second gun from its holster and rammed it against Kenneth's skull. The old man now knelt in submission at his whim, history repeating itself.

"Honey, take it easy. Think of the future," Helena warned.

The future? A horrid mess that abandoned him days ago. Philip once ruled what would be. Now, he was a slave to it. No matter how hard the pain was killed, it still fought on; much like himself, it bred on misfortune – preyed on it.

"Philip, stop this savagery this instant," Hericore ordered.

"Or what? You'll kill me too? Like Sicilla, or Ish? Like your entire squad before I meandered into your diseased life and fixed everything?" Philip mocked through gritted teeth.

"No, I won't harm you, and you won't harm him. You talk of heroics, day in and day out, but now is your time to prove the proud heroism you preach. Be the better man – one of good – and lay down the gun, or follow the call of evil and lie down in a shameful bed of your own creation."

"Your way of leading this quest *is over*. We need control, we need order. The scum that wanders into our employ can't be allowed to walk free," Philip said, ever demanding.

"I agree. You're making it mighty clear what happens when I let the reckless roam and rule." Hericore pointed a claw at him. In all the sweat and heat, covered in sand and dirt, Philip had never felt so cold and offended.

"Me?" he questioned in disgust. "I'm the scum? Ha, you've got to be joking."

The drake's eyes narrowed, and his voice flattened. "I'd never joke at such a claim."

"Well, if I'm such scum, *a lunatic*, then maybe I should act like it? I'll start with this filth!" Philip screamed, clicking back the hammer and grasping the trigger.

"Please," Kenneth begged, at his mercy.

"Know what you're doing, Philip. Think before you act," Hericore said, having the gall to discredit his work further.

"Now that's some advice you should follow, boss. I know what I'm doing. My actions feed and protect every one of you. All you do is plan and plan. Hell, even the word 'plan' has a lesser meaning thanks to you. In the end, all your planning does is get people killed!" Philip shouted.

"And what do you *plan* on doing with Kenneth?" Hericore asked. "Because you seem hell-bent on killing him, also."

"He won't do it. He's just like me," Kenneth added, with an almost disappointed voice. The old man was a sick one, even when faced with a gun's barrel.

"Who the hell do you think you are, Ken? A hero? A good man? Well, guess again, because innocent or not you've got guilt in you. You need catharsis from your terrible deeds, you're just waiting to pop. I can see it."

"You're wrong, Philip. I'm just like you: I'm above killing."

It was another backhanded remark made to undermine him, placing unnecessary limits on his power.

"Above killing? You'd think that of me? That's a frigging joke. I'll show you what I'm capable of, you *fraud*!" Philip said, enraged, his words spitting out onto Kenneth's bloody face.

It was then that he felt Helena place her cold, smooth hand on his heated, shaking arm; even her support was slipping away. Something about her touch was familiar, but corrupted. His Plum was rotting.

"Honey–"

"You too?! Thanks, Plum; ditch me for the pack of wolves, why don't ya," he moaned, a crack appearing in his frail throat.

All the eyes in Declandale were spectators, mocking silently, ever lying, never loyal. "You should never have broken them out, boss. Look what you've done."

"You wanted a breakout, Phil. This is your fault; you're the architect of your own misery. Accept responsibility for once," Hericore said, taking the offensive, backed by the unwashed masses of Karin.

The crowd all cheered for the diplomatic drake, calling for mercy.

"I wanted to release a bunch of psychopaths and fire them at Barsalt. I never wanted to break bread with them – to live beside them. That was all you!" Philip replied, then pointed a finger at each prisoner in turn. "You're all drunken *savages*! Rabid animals that were lucky to be unchained. I regret granting you that privilege."

His grip tightened, as too did his lip; all Hericore did in response was lower his head in disappointment.

"Philip, I..."

"And you're the worst of them. The deadliest by far. But not because of lethality, but for your insufferable lack of action. We've all heard stories from the Great War: platoons lost to your precious *planning*," Philip pressed.

"A lot of sin happened in the war. I can't be blamed for that."

"Okay, what about the more recent examples? I already mentioned Sicilla and Ish. Hell, even that cur Donsis is a victim of YOU!" In a breath, his rage cooled into a jealous and sad tone. "You have all this power, this rapport, and you *squander* it."

Hericore stopped for a moment – a reply lingered, trapped in the drake's devious mind. Thoughts were happening, cogs were turning and contorting in all manner of ways – the terrifying wait of debate.

"Rick was right about you. I shouldn't have traded your trust for his."

"And now we're back to Rick. What'd he say about me? Is he against me too?" Philip replied, exhausting in the sun.

"Rick believed you to be the traitor," Hericore spilled, "and like a proud father, I refused to do anything about it."

It was Philip's turn to twist his mental clock back, and everything started to make sense in his aching, illogical mind. Hericore's own words betrayed Rick and all they stood for. With that sudden epiphany, Philip had to say something most foul – he had to admit his fault.

"No. We're both wrong. It was Kenneth that spoke truths, not lies," Philip reluctantly said.

The 'fisherman' paused.

"I did?"

"Yes, you did. Philip was wrong, as was I. Rick is the one working under the Casterland's command," Hericore agreed. The old drake finally spoke sense, thinking like Philip – it was like a wish come true to the lad.

"The traitor put us against each other to tear us apart," Philip continued, lowering the gun.

"Oh, right. That's not good," Kenneth said, playing along with a perfect performance.

"Why? Where's Rick now?"

"He left... South, I think."

It was then and there that his mission changed. Philip still longed to weed out the traitor and whoever their handler was, but his target had shifted. Rick's rejections now seemed just; the Greycoat had feared his detective talents, and pushed him away from his achievement. For a ploy so devious, Rick earned the top spot upon his list of problems.

If only the lad knew how close his and the Order's fates were. Both were misdirected by the drake, both for their own good. Rick made a convincing villain, and a villain was exactly what Philip needed. Perhaps Hericore wasn't the only fool under the Karinese sun?

"Thank you, Hericore. Maybe you're not completely doomed after all," Philip celebrated, tossing Mercy into the air. He sprinted over to Travis and collected his rations, before passing an order to his one-legged friend.

"Keep watch over these chumps, kid. Don't be afraid to put your foot down too."

"What are you doing?" asked Travis, a question asked again by Helena.

"Simple. I'm going to find Rick, and I'm going to kill him."

"You can't go alone in the desert. The sands alone will tear you up," Helena said.

"Then follow me into hell and back, my sweet plum." He made haste away from the camp and the jovial air of Declandale.

"It's fine, Helena. Follow him," allowed Hericore.

"Philip!" Kenneth called. "Good luck. Killing Rick, I mean."

"I'll need it," Philip cheered, rubbing his sore noggin. "I suppose I'm sorry, old man. Don't expect me to repeat myself, either. Perhaps in time I can make things right with you and the boss. But for now, I've gotta mutt to track down."

The walk from town was met with odd looks from locals, most hearing and fearing his rant. It was a look he needed to adjust to now. Or did he?

True, his mask had fallen; that didn't mean it couldn't be retrieved. The hero he wanted to be wasn't too far from reach yet. Unshackled from the future's foreboding previews and from Hericore's senile idiocy, Philip was free again. Free to be whatever man he chose to be, look how he wanted to look.

After Rick was sorted, to King Barsalt he'd venture. The mission was unchanged, and his visions would be unchanged. All for justice, all for glory, all for the lost lovers and fallen friends that got him this far. Philip was back in his prime.

Chapter 19: Hart the Bold

Hart napped away, wasting half the day, until a thick slap from a meaty hand caught his cheek. Awoken, he was pulled from the coach and dropped the brick roads of Valordolt. With hands bound and weapons removed, wit was all he had left to fend off the ravenous persecution spewing from Dirk's seat atop the city.

Along with Clara, she was all that remained of the Order's higher-ups, and all that stood between him and Kenneth. Having no more patience for either the Council or his escaped mongrel, Hart wanted a swift resolution to today's impediment, one only Boyd could bring, by executing their little Code Black.

Valordolt had been reduced to a husk of what it once was. After the Belmont Bombing, people walked the streets with signs rallying the Order and forcing them to ban magic in the city walls. Aside from alienating one of the world's most powerful forces, they sought to purge all wizards and mages from the land too, adding to the extensive list of things Vitalanders have been taught to hate.

Hart watched suited men walk beside beggars and child march by the old. Being sickened by the show of 'compassion', he couldn't wait to finish what Bart started so long ago. The people on the streets appeared with every tragedy, never holding their caring morality for more than a week. When the Belmont Bombing vanished from memory, they'd all go home and forget all of their compassion.

Outside the Citadel, people were cordoned off by barricades and paladins. Many shock troopers stood with the guard, just waiting for a chance to fry anyone foolish enough to cross the line. They were entering through Belmont, and the missing tower above was somewhat relieving. To know the traitorous Hericore had no home left was a nice thought. If only the grey sky above didn't make things so ominous.

"You're expected upstairs, Hart. Get moving!" said Jovee, the knight that captured him. Without a word, the Warden calmly entered the Citadel and proceeded to the elevator. "You're taking the stairs with me, sunshine."

The knight took joy in controlling him, but not for long. Boyd and Jelz were free to roam, and that wasn't a wise action, given their loyalty.

Thousands of chipped steps were scaled each flight being narrower than the last. Jovee, in his silver suit, found the trip draining. Hart, nice and rested, had no trouble. The view from the Citadel's high point was a beauty still. Unfortunately, this couldn't last. Hart savoured the skyline, committing it to memory as a painting deep within his head, now certain he'd never see the city again.

In the Council's chamber, dismay ruled, and only two seats had members to fill them. Dirk and Clara presided over his return, and neither seemed eager to be there. Dirk, though unhappy to see him, did drip with anticipation over what would become of him, should the Order have their way.

Pulled over the centre sigil, Hart was surrounded by Jovee and three more knights in shining Casterland armour, but varying colour in their capes. Whatever lies Dirk told to earn the Land's support, it was a group effort, with Baie blues, Taurus red, and even Ontarian orange.

Leaning over her desk, Dirk started the festivities with a bitter-sweet, "Welcome home, Warden."

"That's ex-Warden now, Mabel. If you're going to slight me by dragging me back here, at least take a minute to learn the proper etiquette."

She didn't find his retorts any fun, and made a loose verdict.

"Given your confession to Jovee, I say we should let you hang." The knights clamped his arms, prepared to remove him from court. "Oh, and skip the jail time. We all know how careless the boys can be with keys in that place."

"Wait! I deserve to defend myself. My confession was a tad exaggerated," Hart called.

Dirk didn't reply, only yawning in response. But Clara still believed in the 'proper' protocols and gave him a chance. Waving away the knights, she whimpered.

"Please, step forward, and clear your name. For both our sakes." The girl seemed at the end of her wits, losing much over the last few days; the Order really lost itself when Hericore jumped ship.

Under the rising quarter moon, Hart let the cool air flow throughout before starting to stall. The night's light had just past over Dirk's shoulder, and when it struck his own, time would be upon them both.

"Would either of you lovely ladies believe me if I claimed to be innocent?" he asked, slowly.

Clara's decision came just as slowly, and Dirk played with the stationery upon her neat desk, giving no thought to the question.

Folding up paper figurines, Dirk answered with, "No, not really, love."

"Do you have evidence to prove that point?" Hart countered.

As if this question would assuredly be asked, Jovee held up the Warden's rifle. The knight was proud to please his mistress – or to engorge his pay.

"The shot pulled from Hunter's back was from your gun. That's evidence enough," the knight smirked.

"I didn't shoot that gun, not once. That was an assassin, hired to kill Hunter. The Holy Blade, Kalsec."

Mention of his name would be enough to plunge any sane person into fear, but caring little for it, Dirk never flinched.

"Kalsec's not here… not in Valordolt, is he?" Clara asked Dirk, shaken.

"I hope so. He's on the payroll. I'd hate to fire the poor chap."

Being under the Order's thumb would explain the knowledge the assassin held, but didn't feel right. Killing with years of premeditation, that was how the Ripper operated, and Kalsec was no different; their likeness sat uneasy in Hart's stomach.

"You can't handle a man of Kalsec's stature. He'd swallow this city whole, if it pleased him," Hart said.

"Once, yes," agreed Dirk. "But that was the old Kalsec. Now, the old man has found repentance in our ranks. You should have joined him long ago."

"How does a killer find any home in this Order? We give life, not take it!"

The moonlight moved further across the room, and Hart's struggle to find innovative distractions was running thin.

"Kalsec isn't a killer, not anymore. He welcomed a peace vow and joined the bell-ringers below us," Dirk explained.

Those who grew old in the Order and survived a lifetime of warring became one of two things: Ringers or Singers. Singers were ten a penny, and manned the choirs across hundreds of churches. But the Ringers? Ringers were one in million.

Removed from society, removed from humanity, and given one goal – manning the Citadel's clock tower – Ringers lost their lives, and kept on serving the church. The ever faithful were conditioned to never leave the tower – they stayed through fearful want, not need. The ties that bound a Ringer would be loose indeed.

The bells of Valordolt tolled by the quarter of each hour, but when the city was in danger, a special chime was tolled.

"The bells that tolled on Cinquiday night. You heard them ringing, I assume?" Hart asked the Council.

"Living so close has raised my tolerance for such sound," Clara replied.

"I heard them. Midnight's tolls, and nothing more," Dirk added.

"No. There was plenty more. The bells rang, and the paladins from my prison frenzied; they turned on us, killed the hunters," Hart argued intently.

"Poppycock. The Ringer must consult us before uttering a Call to Action."

Her ignorance was matched only by Hart's patience for such a thing. Luckily, the light still continued its passage, and she was allowed to ramble further.

"The only frenzy that occurred the night was orchestrated by you, Percival. Witnesses saw you cleaving the men apart," she continued to spew.

Kalsec had painted a rather convincing picture of Hart's madness – all while he walked away with a single bullet wound. But even when marked by legend, Hart didn't yield.

"You know what, I admit it. I killed them all; Hunter too... *especially* Hunter," Hart cheered, looking to the sky. "You win, Mabel. You and Kalsec have beaten me. But I'm not the one you must seek. In a world of shambling corpses, vicious beasts, and cut-throat killers, Kenneth is the worst of them all."

The truth caused Clara to gasp and drop back into her cushions, as with the unveiling of Hericore's true colours. The girl was frail, too frail for this world.

"I've watched you grow into a monster too, Percival, seething with an undying lust for revenge. Even with your 'Ripper' under your own roof, you still never reaped his life. You don't want to because his continued existence is an excuse for your dark deeds," concluded Dirk, unleashing years of bottled opinions onto him.

"I do what most can't, not because I'm driven to darkness, but because darkness drives to me," Hart corrected her. "I'm a man who can do the unthinkable to stop the criminal horde from ruling this frail land."

Dirk snorted. "How self-indulgent. Any last words, m'dear?"

"A warning: it's too late to save the Order, but let me go, and I can save you." The Warden made this offer with the utmost sincerity, void of his previous joy.

"And you claim to be free of darkness? I pity you... I'm almost sorry about what happens next. Take him away, boys. Finally, I can sleep." But, as Dirk flicked her wrist, the moon's gaze hit Hart's eye, and the fun began. The night sky lit up in a bright orange flash, and anarchy's true colours shone through.

A thunderous boom consumed their ears, followed by screams, distant and plenty. The knights panicked, as did Dirk. The look on the Banker's face was the last memento he kept from Valordolt; victory had found him, at last.

"What was that?!" Clara screamed.

"That, my dear, was change," Hart said. "It's a shame. I honestly didn't want this. But hiring a man like Kalsec, then having the gall to pin Belmont on me? That's too far. So I hope you'll understand."

"For better..." Boyd said, entering the chamber.

"...Or worse," Jelz followed. "'Bout time we got the ball rolling."

Hart was soon snapped free from his bindings and free to join another round of combat, full of wrath and lustful bile. After wiping out the Fork's fighters, the silver knights were a joke for the trio, and soon the room was clear of hostile swords.

"It's about time you showed up, Reltus," Hart thanked the molluskan.

"That candle was awful tricky to set up."

The knights' blood pooled over the Order's golden heart, soaking into the marble's cracks and staining it a deep red, a heart's true appearance. More explosive sounds filled the sky, but of a different kind. Thunder and lightning came with a storm of rain; a flash flood that poured off the glass ceiling, and caused fluid shadows to dance across the hall's floor.

"What's going on here?!" Dirk furiously belted out. "What could you morons possibly hope to achieve?"

"Simple. We want to end this pathetic attempt at 'order'," Hart said.

"We do?" asked Jelz.

"No, but while we're here."

"My family will be safe, right? Hiding below ground?" Boyd wondered.

"It worked for Hericore. The Guard had their little basement, and we have the Vault."

Crying at the bloody scene, Clara begged for her life, offering everything from roths to the very virginity half of Valordolt longed for. Nicknames meant a lot to a person's character, and Hart had no intention to rob Clara of hers.

"You can leave her unscathed – both of you. We're not the bad guys," he told the women. "But the thousands of criminals we just released might not be so kind."

"No. You didn't..." said a hopeless Dirk. The haggard Banker also shed some tears, ones much sweeter than Clara's. Hart had no guilt over sending her to an untimely end; the witch deserved to burn for denying him vengeance.

"Yes. It's Bart all over again. And this time, I won't be around to solve your problems." Looking over the dead, the Warden smiled. "Let's hope Wellington's home soon."

"We'll survive, you know," Dirk said, shivering. "We'll chase you down and end you!"

"Who will be left to give chase? You? I dread to imagine the months you'll spend writing Black Letters after tonight, Mabel," Hart replied, before strolling out of their chambers into the brave new world he'd help forge.

The streets were full of degenerates killing, stealing, raping, burning, bashing, boozing, and crying for forgiveness. The world burned around them as the three rode for Karin, free from order. Animals ran the city now, and Hart wasn't lingering in hopes of joining the herd. Bart's dreams had come true, and he couldn't afford to bask in the anarchy.

Riding past the opera house, it remained silent, but he still heard a wondrous tune made by his own hand, backed by bells and harmonised in screams, a lust for acceptance beat on in his head.

It drummed and drummed, becoming the twisted call to action that he longed for. A tune with such propulsion could inspire anyone to rule Magnus. All Hart wanted was that which was stolen from him... His family.

Epilogue

Hericore watched a dark creature slither away, wearing Philip like a shell, and shattering the Drakeguard before his tired eyes. It was true that his order had fallen days ago – beginning with Travis and Harlan's injuries, it was only bolstered by Lucille's breakdown and Haruka's exile.

But now, with a trusted friend storming away, chasing a ghost across Karin and dragging his manipulated girl along, made Hericore realise the destruction he'd brokered.

It was a good deed for him and Kenneth to lie to Philip, sparing both their lives and Rick’s. But still, it’d cost them the dandy boy's own soul.

A second chance was an uncommon term for a dragon. Most draconic law dismissed the rule, and this spawned Hericore’s own reliance on it – for anyone who couldn’t forgive was truly lost.

With hope in his heart, he chased Philip into the wilderness. If a boy so naïve could forgive others, then he was not lost. Then maybe he could forgive Philip for today's rude accusations and, in turn, find redemption; one big circle of acceptance.

This was a big ask, though. When he’d first met Philip, he’d fought for the hero within the boy, a struggle that would be increased now, amidst the strain of playing saviour. He held full responsibility for this, moulding Philip into a self-confident savant, poised to save the world. The entirety of Magnus and Prime was balanced on their shoulders – not a fun time for anyone.

Still, Hericore was willing and able, and so Philip could be too. Rick was wrong about the cocky kid – he wasn't a threat, not if Hericore still had breath to draw. Hope remained.

He lamented leaving the others in Declandale, forcing them to find their own passage south. But they weren't broken like Philip – collectively they weren't.

An ever solid judge of character, he knew Kenneth to be strong, stronger than he let on. It was another one of his gut feelings – like with Philip – and never had such instincts proved him wrong.

Few of the Drakeguard were even alive when Kenneth was incarcerated, and the drake luckily was one of them. Acting as ignorant as they come back then, the terms of Kenneth's arrest had been hazy to him, and the newly appointed Warden outright forced the arrest onto the Order's justice system.

Hericore knew of Kenneth's crimes, but never believed in them. Many a murderer had worn convincing disguises of innocence over the years, and Kenneth wasn't one of them; his innocent claims must be genuine.

The meeting of himself, Philip and Kenneth was no accident or luck. As Philip used to say, there is no true luck. Whatever pushed them together, be it the gods, primal stones, or something else entirely, it was good news. Since their paths collided, the curse that was destined to kill him was easing. It didn't reverse, but thankfully slowed.

Prophecies were another silly concept to dragons, but just this once, Hericore believed otherwise. For the salvation began with the meeting of the minds.

–Fin–

Special Thanks

This project wouldn't have been possible without the backing and support of some amazing individuals.

These special people are:

Allistair 'AJ' Morne

Brent Skinner

Danny Goldsmith

Eleanor Joyce

Genine

Henry Double

Holden Stenner

Mark Armstrong Allard

Maureen Robinson

Michael Grover

Pat Barker

Steph Sayer

Appendix

The Drakeguard Knights:

–Hericore, Arch-Paladin, head of the Order's High Council

–Philip, former Vagabond, Hericore's ward

–Zarpadon, the fallen angel and Hericore's personal assistant

–Helena Starr, former Vagabond, captain of Hericore's Guard

–Bella Starr, Helena's pet bird.

–Ashley 'Ash' Belwert, member of the Guard

–Travis Farland, former Vagabond, Hericore's cleric and doctor

–Thomas Tel-Moot, former Vagabond, member of the Guard

– James Stone, former Vagabond, member of the Guard

–Krell, member of the Guard?

–Gerald, horse of the Guard

–Bella, bird belonging to Helena

The Escapee Prisoners:

–Kenneth Porter, former Central Block prisoner and fisherman with a limited skill set

–Lucille Woodward, former East Block prisoner and hunter, sought for her survival skills

–Harlan Ainsworth, former West Block prisoner and legend, sought for his array of knowledge

–Hemora Vangesh, former West Block prisoner and nobleman, sough for his combat abilities

–Haruka Katowa, former East Block prisoner and assassin, sought for her deceptive talents

–Randell 'Rangar' Garwood-Edwards, former West Block prisoner and mercenary, sought for his combat abilities

–Donsis Allisteel, former West Block prisoner and loan shark, sought for his wealth

Members of the Order:

–Royland, Father, founder of the Order

–Mabel Dirk, Head Banker of the High Council

–Clara Cristel, Cardinal of the High Council

–Ryon Wellington, Battlemaster of the High Council

–Matthias Gilligan, Saint of the High Council

–Percival Hart, Warden of Refracted Light

–Boyd Loyce, Captain of Refracted Light

–Jelz Reltus, Captain of Refracted Light

–Lud Kavel, Paladin under Hart's command

–Hunter, head hunter for the Order

–Daniels, Paladin under Hunter's command

–William Kavel, squire to Ryon Wellington

–Stanley, member of the Order

–Phineas, member of the Order

Other Characters:

–Xander Greenhill, former Lord of the Green Isles

–Kalsec, the Moonsabre, mysterious stranger

–Mary, servant of Theoline

–Edgar Svanold, Mayor of Brideport

–Boris, patron at Trawlers Inn

–Catherine, member of the Wild Cats

–Katherine, member of the Wild Cats

–Gaffer, leader of the Wild Cats

–Opyus, leader of Vipsa

–Bol, member of Vipsa

–Langdon, travelling knight

–The Stranger, member of the Declandale Bandits

–Pavlov, a potion seller from Karin

–Patrick 'Ricky' Morello, Greycoat detective

–Madame Osiris, leader of the Cult of Undying

–Natalia, granddaughter to Osiris

–Dallas, patchwork soldier working under Natalia

–The Beast, patchwork soldier working under Natalia

–The Trapmaster, legendary master of mind control

Gods of Prime:

–Gideon, Great Lord, God of Power, leader of the Primals

–Theoline the Wise, God of Knowledge, Valentine's brother

–Valentine, Mother, Goddess of Love, Gideon's wife

–Bethany the Blessed, Goddess of Life, daughter of Gideon and Valentine

–Lilith, The Reaper, Goddess of Death, daughter of Gideon and Valentine

–Aldrich the Forsaken, God of Undeath, son of Gideon and Valentine

–Aldon, God of the Arcane, creator of elves, banished

–Solaris, God of the Sun, banished

–Luna, Goddess of the Moon, sister to Solaris

–Hugo, Patriarch of Man, God of Jealousy and Fear, creator of mankind

Locations:

–Magnus, land of mortals

–Midgartt, central continent of Magnus

–Vitalands, land of the Order, located in west Midgartt

–Valordolt, capital of the Vitalands

–Bridgeport, city in the Vitalands

–Betiel, city in the Vitalands

–Ryford, city in the Vitalands

–Convict's Cove, town in the Vitalands

–Lumber's End, town in the Vitalands

–Roy's Fork, Village in the Vitalands

–Igial's Lane, Hamlet in the Vitalands

–Casterlands, land of the Caster Council, located in east Midgartt

–Karin Freelands, land of the lawless, located in south-west Midgartt

–Declandale, frontier town in the Freelands

–East Karin, land of the desert dwarves, located in south-east Midgartt

–Barsameil, land of the Barsalt Dynasty, located in far south Midgartt

–Arcwoods, land of the Birch Dynasty, located in north Midgartt

–Ivory Helm, land of the Helm Lordship, located in far north Midgartt–Eastock, the eastern continent of Magnus

–Wasternlands, the western continent of Magnus

–Tealka, the underwater continent of Magnus, under the ocean between Midgartt and Eastock

–Prime, land of the gods

–Etheriam, the waters of heaven

–Tarus, the pits of hell

Items of Importance:

–Time Stone, Tempus Porta, able to manipulate the flow of time, currently in the Drakeguard's possession

–Space Stone, Raumtür, able to manipulate the fabric of reality, whereabouts unknown

–Mind Stone, Mentir Mania, able to manipulate another's perception, whereabouts unknown

–Matter Stone, Yugo Materia, able to transmute any material into another, currently in King Barsalt's possession

–Pyrus, an elemental crystal of condensed heat energy, used by Harlan

–Arcus, an elemental crystal of condensed arcane energy, the material crystivines are made from

–Rouge Candle, a magical remote detonator for arcos runes, build by Bart the Bold, currently in Hart's possession

–Arcos Rune, a magically powered clay explosive

–Rouge Candle, magically-powered remote detonator used by Bart the Bold

–Ale of Amnesia, potion that can erase memories

Also By Jack Robinson

The Tales of Magnus and Prime: Meeting of the Minds Volume 1

The Tales of Magnus and Prime: Meeting of the Minds Volume 2

The Prequels of Magnus and Prime: Kadian

Smile

Room 3B-1

Available online now, for free. Check out:

magnusandprime.com

for more.

36092838R00092

Printed in Great Britain
by Amazon